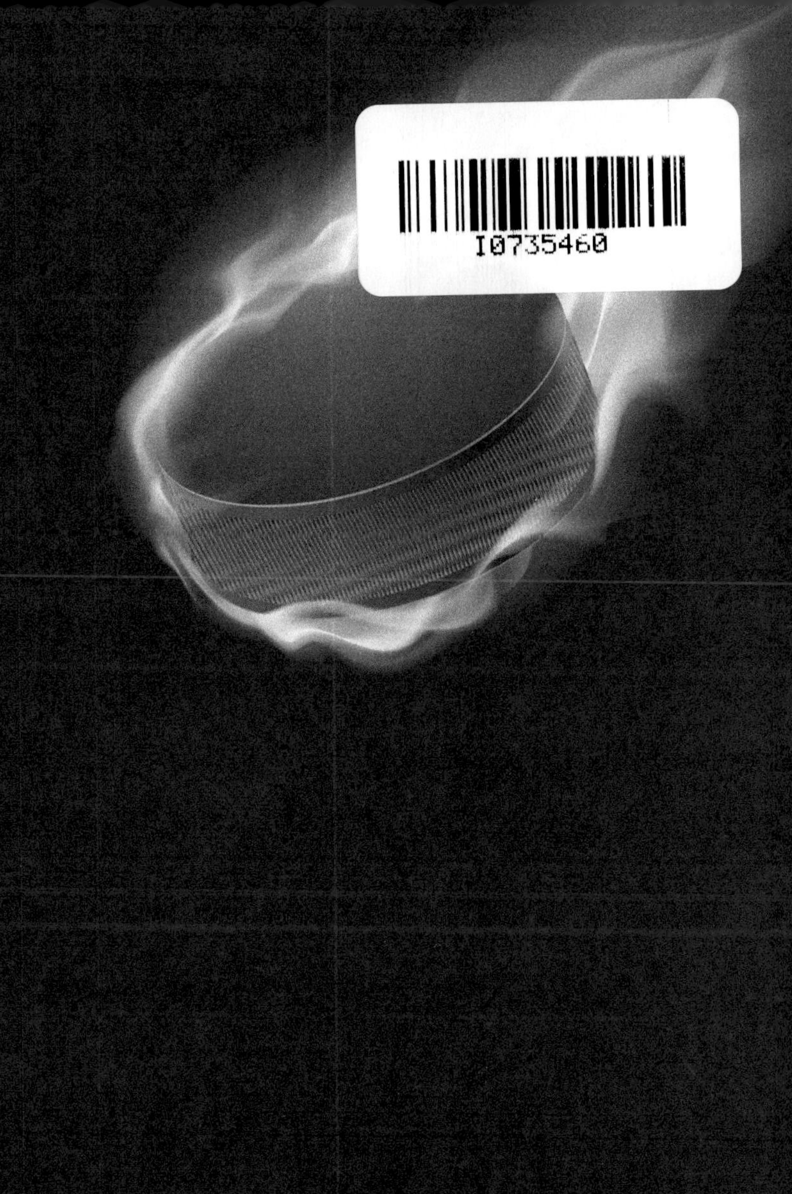

PUCKS & PENALTIES
A compilation of outtakes and deleted scenes from The Pucked
Series

From PUCKED

ENDORSE THIS: an Area 51 invasion outtake in which Alex once
again tries to persuade Violet that he should go where no man has
gone before. And likely never will. Also includes outtakes such
as Weiner Warmers: a Holiday Outtake, Let's Make An Alex Jr,
Pretty Eyes (a Pucked Good Luck Charm crossover), MILF in
Training and Kick Stand Kid.

From PUCKED OFF

A Valentine's Day love note, a series of deleted, never before seen
scenes from the cutting room floor of Pucked Off and a special
birthday outtake.

From PUCKED LOVE

The original Prologue that didn't make the cut in Pucked Love and
a Valentine's Day letter from Darren to Charlene that will make
you swoon.

PRAISE FOR HELENA HUNTING'S NOVELS

"Characters that will touch your heart and a romance that will leave you breathless."

-New York Times bestselling author Tara Sue Me

"Gut wrenching, sexy, twisted, dark, incredibly erotic and a love story like no other. On my all-time favorites list."

-Alice Clayton, *New York Times* bestselling author of *Wallbanger* and The Redhead series

"A look into the world of tattoos and piercings, a dash of humor and a feel-good ending will delight fans and new readers alike."

-Publishers Weekly (on *Inked Armor*)

"A unique, deliciously hot, endearingly sweet, laugh out loud, fantastically good time romance!! . . . I loved every single page!!"

—New York Times Bestselling author Emma Chase on *PUCKED*

"Sigh inducing swoony and fanning myself sexy. All the stars!"

-USA Today bestselling author Daisy Prescott on The Pucked Series

"A hot rollercoaster of a ride!"

-Julia Kent, *New York Times* and *USA Today* bestselling author on *Pucked Over*

"*Pucked Over* is Helena Hunting's funniest and sexiest book yet. SCORCHING HOT with PEE INDUCING LAUGHS. All hail the Beaver Queen."

-T. M. Frazier, *USA Today* bestselling author

TITLES BY HELENA HUNTING

PUCKED SERIES
Pucked (Pucked #1)
Pucked Up (Pucked #2)
Pucked Over (Pucked #3)
Forever Pucked (Pucked #4)
Pucked Under (Pucked #5)
Pucked Off (Pucked #6)
Pucked Love (Pucked #7)
AREA 51: Deleted Scenes & Outtakes
Get Inked (A crossover novella)

THE CLIPPED WINGS SERIES
Cupcakes and Ink
Clipped Wings
Between the Cracks
Inked Armor
Cracks in the Armor
Fractures in Ink

SHACKING UP SERIES
Shacking Up
Getting Down (Novella)
Hooking Up
I Flipping Love You
Handle with Care (Summer 2019)

STANDALONE NOVELS
The Librarian Principle
Felony Ever After

FOREVER ROMANCE STANDALONES
The Good Luck Charm
Meet Cute

PUCKS & PENALTIES

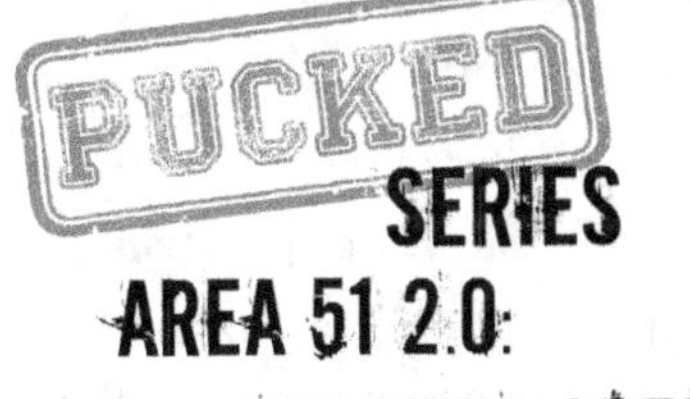

SERIES

AREA 51 2.0:
OUTTAKES & DELETED SCENES

Published by Helena Hunting

Cover art design by Shanoff Designs
Cover font from Imagex Fonts
Cover image from depositphoto.com
Formatting by CP Smith
Editing by Paige Maroney Smith
Proofing by the Hustlers

DEDICATION

Huge love and thanks to my awesome Hustlers for beta reading this pile of crazy. To Teeny for formatting this, to Jenn for giving me a way to get it to you without forcing you to read it on your phone or a computer screen, and to Sarah for being so willing to drop everything and read.

Thank you, readers, for loving these two. You're the reason I've been able to make my dream a reality. I hope you have as much fun reading as I did writing this insanity. Enough rambling. Go get your Violet and Alex fix.

#VioletIsMySpiritAnimal

Why did I write this nonsense? It was for the anniversary of Pucked and I felt like revisiting these insane characters and giving Alex a little of the forbidden fruit. Also, Violet is just fun to write, and whenever I'm struggling with character voices, I can always come back to these two and they feel real and natural and easy. So I wrote this bag of ridiculous to go with all the other ridiculousness.

I PULL INTO THE garage, retrieve my hockey bag from the trunk and bring it straight to the laundry room. My equipment smells like dirty ball sac—Violet's description—and she gets annoyed when I leave it to fester in the front foyer. I toss the washable items into the machine and set them to soak.

Normally, I'd leave all this stuff for the housekeeper, but I need my equipment tomorrow and she won't be here until later in the week. I'm also trying to win bonus points with my wife. The kind that might result in sexual favors. It's a busy time of year at work for her, so my Super Cock and me do not have top spot on her to-do list.

Also, smelly hockey equipment is not a turn-on, or so I've been told. It's interesting how things change, particularly over the past two years, since we got caught fucking in the locker room. Back then she blew me straight off the ice. Now if I try to get a little action after a run or practice, I'm sent straight to the shower. She joins me, of course, but I get several cursory seconds alone under the spray to wash off most of the sweat first. I don't really mind, because she typically performs a strip tease during that time and then presses her boobs against the glass, which I appreciate.

Today, I'm returning from practice showered and wearing fresh clothes that were not occupying the same bag as my hockey equipment. Again, mixing fresh laundry and stinky hockey equipment equals delayed gratification. I have two hours before I have to leave for a meeting with my agent to discuss a few potential endorsement options, and Violet is working from home today.

Later, Darren and Charlene are coming over for dinner—it's supposed to be a short break in Violet's otherwise tight schedule, and after food I've been told she and Charlene have reports they need to review. My current plan is to capitalize on this small window of spare time by enticing Violet to break for lunch—a naked lunch, unless she's in the middle of something. Violet can be difficult to distract when she's mathing, which is entirely possible since she hasn't come to greet me in the minutes I've been home.

I don't call out to let her know I'm here; I'm banking on the element of surprise. I check the most obvious places first, like the kitchen and the living room—sometimes she brings her laptop down when she gets tired of her office, or if it's nice out she'll work by the pool. She's in none of these locations, so I have to assume she's upstairs in her office.

Muffled bass grows louder as I ascend the stairs. Her office door is open and her back is to me, hair pulled up into a loose ponytail as she types away on her computer, humming tunelessly to the song blasting from the sound system. When it gets to a part she knows, she stops typing and belts out the lyrics while shimmying in her chair. As soon as the chorus is over, she goes back to humming and her fingers return to the keyboard. I have to bite the inside of my cheek to keep from laughing.

I'm about to announce my presence when the doorbell rings. Violet rolls her chair back and spins around.

Gripping the armrests, she shrieks. "What the fuck, Alex?"

"Sorry. I just got home."

"So you thought you'd scare the shit out of me?" She pushes up out of the chair and presses a palm against her chest, drawing my attention to her boobs, or at least the exceptional amount of cleavage. She's wearing a loose tank with my team logo. It has a sheer quality to it, through which I can see the camisole and bra she's wearing underneath. There are excessive straps and not enough nipple visibility.

"How long have you been standing there?"

"Not long."

She gives me the stink eye and moves to step past me, but I block her way.

"Someone's at the door."

"I'll get it." I cup her boobs and lean down to kiss her frowning mouth.

"Is this why you came up here? Just to cop a feel?" she says against my lips.

"I came up to say hi and to see if you wanted to have

lunch with me before I meet with my agent this afternoon." I brush my thumbs over her nipples. They're barely detectible through the layers of cotton, satin, and padding.

The doorbell rings a second time and she pushes my hands away. "My boobs will still be here after whoever's at the door is gone."

I step in front of her, intent on getting there first. It's okay for me to check out her awesome cleavage, not so much the FedEx guy—if that's even who it is. It better not be some solicitor. Violet follows me downstairs and waits behind me as I unlock the door and greet the delivery person—who happens to be female. And older. Like my mother's age. She hands me a box wrapped in non-descript packaging with a look that screams judgment. I ignore her disapproval and tuck the package under my arm, glancing over my shoulder at Violet, who's peeking out from behind me.

"Make any purchases you want to tell me about?" I ask.

Occasionally, Violet uses my credit card to buy things when she's too lazy to find her purse. Last time I opened a package containing new lingerie and ruined her surprise. It had my name on it, so it wasn't really my fault and I still enjoyed seeing her in it.

She crosses her arms over her chest and glances pointedly at the black plastic wrapped package. "No. Have you?"

"Not unless I've been sleep-shopping." I sign for it, thank the delivery lady, and close the door.

As soon as I turn around, Violet makes a grab for the box. I raise it over my head and enjoy watching her boobs bounce as she jumps for it. It's even better when she holds onto my shoulders and tries to climb my body to reach it.

"You ordered something from a porn site! I want to see what it is!"

I give her a hand by holding onto her ass and lifting her higher so her boobs are almost in my face, but the package remains out of reach. "I didn't order this, and why do you assume it's from a porn site?"

"Because it's in black packaging with no logo on it. Only porn stuff comes in packages like that."

"And how would you know that?" I lower her until her feet hit the floor.

"Because I've ordered from an online porn shop before." She holds out her arms, but does it in such a way that she squeezes her boobs together. "Gimme."

I hand over the box. I'm actually quite curious, since I haven't ordered anything from an online porn shop recently. I would definitely remember if I had.

Violet hugs the box to her chest and runs down the hall, into the kitchen. Pulling a pair of scissors from the drawer, she carefully cuts through the tape and pries the flaps apart, tossing air-filled packing bags onto the counter.

Her brow comes down and her lips follow in a frown as she takes in the contents.

"What is it?" I step up behind her with the intention of looking over her shoulder, and maybe rubbing on her a little.

She spins away, the object—whatever it is—clutched to her chest in one hand as she skitters around the opposite side of the kitchen island. "Are you serious with this, Alex?"

Shit. She looks pissed. And maybe a tad bit nervous. And also just the wee-est bit excited—or it's possible the last part is just me projecting the kind of reaction I'd like to see to new sex stuff—if that's what it is. Now I really want to know what the hell was in that box.

I side-step right.

Violet points an accusatory finger at me and shuffles in the opposite direction, maintaining our distance. "Stay right the fuck there, Alex. If you come one step closer, I swear to God you will never touch my boobs again."

"Baby, I don't know what's got you so worked up, but I assure you, whatever you're holding, I didn't order it."

Violet scoffs. "That's complete and utter bullshit." She slams not one, but two items on the counter with such force that they bounce and one rolls toward me. I catch it as it falls over the edge.

"I know what that is! Don't think I don't!" Her voice is high and pitchy.

I read the label and suddenly her extreme reaction is much less confusing. I'm holding a bottle of lube. But not just any kind of lube. Anal lube. "I don't know where this came from, but I didn't buy it."

"Ha! I don't believe you!"

"It's not like I can just unsuspectingly sneak things into your ass, Violet."

"You've snuck a finger in there before!" It's an accusation. She also moves a hand behind her, as if she's gone into ass-protection mode.

I raise a brow. "I didn't sneak it in there. I made it very clear what I was planning to do, and gave you every opportunity to say no thank you." I reach for the second package, which is still on the counter, NS realize it's a butt plug.

She nabs it before I can, which is shocking, because normally Violet's reaction time is much slower than mine. She waves it around in the air manically. "And this! What were you planning on doing with this?"

It's hard not to laugh, but I'm aware if I do, I'm likely going to be taking care of my own hard-ons for a while. My hands are not soft like Violet's, so I keep my expression calmly neutral.

"Baby, I have no plans for that because I didn't buy it. Maybe it's a prank. Maybe Charlene sent it." I make a mental note to thank her if that's the case.

"Ha!" she barks. "Why would she send me this—" The packaged butt plug flies out of her waving hand. I make a quick shift to the right and snatch it out of the air. "—when I already have almost the exact same one?"

I fumble the package. "What the what? You what?" Her eyes flare with panic as mine narrow.

"Nothing. Never mind."

"You can't backtrack when you say something like that, Violet. Since when do you have one of these?" I hold up the plug. It seems pretty nice as far as plugs go—although my only references are from porn since getting near Violet's No-Go Zone is so rare that I'd never anticipated needing one. The end is all fancy, with what at first appears to be a jewel. On closer inspection, I realize it's the team logo. What the hell? Since when do we have Chicago-based sex toys? And who's the fucking genius behind that idea?

Just the possibility of using this is giving me one hell of a rager, because I'm thinking about the very select times in the past couple of years that I've managed to get in a finger in Violet's Area 51. Even if she doesn't want to admit she likes it, she's come every single time I've slipped a digit in the back door.

Her eyes dart around the room. I can practically see her wheels turning, as if she's trying to come up with a plausible story, which is pointless, since Violet is the worst liar in the history of the world. If she committed a felony, she would spend the rest of her life in prison, because Violet would confess in two seconds.

"It was a gag gift."

"A gag gift? Who gives someone a butt plug as a joke?"

She cringes at the words *butt plug* and protects her ass again. "Or like a party favor. I don't know. Charlene has weird ideas about what makes an acceptable gift."

"Charlene gave you a butt plug?"

"Well, who else do I know who would gift me an Area 51 invasion implement? Other than my mother, but even that's a little outside of her realm of inappropriateness." She's doing that flail thing with her hands—like she does when she's nervous.

Violet's sufficiently distracted that she hasn't noticed me moving around the island. "When did Charlene give you a butt plug?"

That gets me another shudder. "What?" Now she's playing with the end of her ponytail.

"The butt plug. When did she give it to you?"

Violet shrugs. "A while ago."

"What's a while ago?"

She mumbles something I don't quite catch.

"What was that?"

"When we were in Vegas." It's still mumbled, but I can understand her this time.

Now it's my turn to frown. "You've had a butt plug since Vegas?" That's nearly a year ago.

"She gave one to all of us. I forgot all about it until now, when this one showed up." She motions to the one still in my hand.

"To all of you?"

"Yes. All of us got one. Me, Sunny, Lily, and Charlene—well, not Charlene because I'm assuming she already has one, or probably more than one realistically, but she felt like she needed to buy one for the rest of us so we could join the Area 51 brigade or whatever. I have no idea. Maybe she wants to start a club. Apparently, she's a big, huge fan of Darren's dick in her Exit Only orifice."

"Charlene and Darren have anal?" That's news to me.

"Don't say that word!" Violet snaps.

"What word? Anal?"

She shivers. "Stop saying that."

Violet's reactions to this topic are highly entertaining. It's difficult not to laugh at her when she's freaking out like this. "Okay, fine. I'll stop saying the 'A' word. But you're telling me Darren gets in the back door?" I can't believe he's never mentioned it, not once. But then, Darren is pretty quiet about what happens behind closed doors with Charlene. Based on some of the things Violet has said, it might be a little on the right side of kinky with those two, which could account for his secrecy on the subject. He's also a private guy.

"That's what she's led me to believe. I'm assuming that means he's not hung, or at least not hung the way you are, unless she previously had a career in porn that I don't know about."

I shrug. "He's not small." We all walk around the locker room naked. Junk is junk.

Violet holds up a hand. "I already know more than I'd like about their anal antics. I have no interest in knowing the dimensions of Darren's doodle."

"So you can say anal and I can't?"

"When you say it, your voice gets all low and growly, like you're thinking about an invasion." She glances at the plug in my hand. "Can you please put that thing down? Just looking at it is making me anxious."

"It's still in the packaging, Violet. It's not going to bite you."

"And that's exactly where it's going to stay, so don't get any ideas."

I hold my fingers up and wiggle them. "It's not like it's any different than these."

She snatches it out of my hand and waves it in my face. "This is more like two fingers, not just one!"

"It's more like my thumb, and I bet you could take two, especially now that we have that lube."

Violet's mouth drops open and she pokes me in the chest, still waving the butt plug around. "I can practically see you scheming, Alex. You think if you can get something like this in there, then the next logical step is the Super MC, but they're not even remotely similar. That's like comparing a Slim Jim to a bratwurst!"

"You're exaggerating again, Violet. My cock is not that big."

"Really, Alex?" She slaps the butt plug on the counter and aggressively pulls at the button on my pants, then roughly unzips the fly. She yanks my pants and boxers down enough so that my cock pops out. "Why are you so hard right now?"

I give her a look. "Because we're talking about sex."

"Butt sex! Why does ass invasion warrant this kind of reaction? Why do you have to be so excited about the prospect?" She squeezes my cock as if to demonstrate how much my excitement annoys her. "Super MC is like level five hard right now. I don't buy for a second that you didn't order this."

She releases my cock and starts fighting with the packaging. Once the plug is free, she grips it in her fist and shakes her hand in front of my face. "Look at this!"

"I'm looking, baby." My voice is low, gritty—I suppose she's right about my tone when we're discussing things like this.

She glares at me. "Don't sex voice me right now, Alex."

"I'm not sex voicing you on purpose. You were just touching my cock. I can't help that it makes me excited."

"It's the Area 51 talk that's making you excited." It an accusation.

"Well, yeah, baby. It's like my unicorn, and you're all worked up, and touching me, and pissed off and I think, if you're honest with yourself, you're turned on and just a little curious."

"I am not!"

"Then why are your cheeks so flushed? And why are your nipples hard?" I brush one with my thumb. It was just a guess, but I'm right, I can feel it pebbling through her bra.

She slaps my hand away. "They're not hard and I'm flushed because we're arguing and you bought Area 51 stuff from an online sex store."

"I swear, I didn't order this stuff." I pry the plug from her fist and set it on the counter.

"Well, where the hell did it come from?"

I switch tactics, because I need her to calm down and relax. I would also like to be able to do something constructive with this hard-on of mine. "I don't know. Maybe it was sent by mistake." I sweep her ponytail over her shoulder. "Violet, have I ever pushed you to do something you didn't want to?"

She purses her lips and then sighs dramatically. "Well . . ."

I arch a brow as I trail my finger from her shoulder up the side of her neck. It makes her eyelids flutter. "Have I?"

"No," she reluctantly admits.

"Exactly. So do you really think I'd order Area 51 stuff when I know this is the kind of reaction I'm going to get?" I'd like to pull her closer, but if I do, I'll jab her in the stomach with my hard-on, which is still hanging out of my pants.

"That still doesn't explain how it magically got mailed to you."

I glance at the bottle of lube. It's from the same company I did a condom endorsement for. "Maybe it has something to do with the endorsement contracts my agent wants me to review. Maybe she thinks she's being funny."

"You are not doing an endorsement for anal lube, Alex. Then people will think I let you in my ass with your extra large cock all the time."

"No, they won't."

She props a fist on her hip. "Oh yes, they will. Everyone believes you have a huge dick because you did that XL condom promo and that milk advertisement in just a pair of underwear—and while that assumption is actually accurate, the last thing I want is people to think you're parking that bus in my butt!"

"That's quite the image you're painting, sweetheart, and as much as my ego appreciates it, you're doing that exaggerating thing again."

"It's not an exaggeration. You're a monster!" She grabs hold of my hanging cock again. "Look at my fingers, Alex. Look at the gap between my finger and thumb!"

"I'm looking." I'm back to that low, gravelly voice.

"I don't have small hands."

"They're small compared to mine." I cover her fingers with my own and encourage her to squeeze.

"This is serious," she says, but her voice lacks its former conviction. Instead, it's softer and just the tiniest bit breathless.

"I agree, and I promise you I won't endorse anything you're not comfortable with." I keep up the slow, easy strokes, sweeping our thumbs over the head as I take a step closer.

"Alex." Now it's just a whisper.

I caress her cheek with my free hand, then skim her bottom lip with my thumb. I dip my head, and when my mouth is a breath away from hers, I murmur, "I'm sorry this freaked you out."

She sighs. "I'm sorry if I overreacted. You know it just makes me nervous."

"Would I ever do anything to hurt you?" I brush my lips over hers.

She swallows hard, fingertips slipping into the hair at the nape of my neck. "No."

"Don't I always make you feel good?" I trail gentle fingers over her breasts, still covered in layers of fabric. I'm going to fix that soon. I just need her slightly more relaxed.

"Yes."

"That's right, baby. That's all I ever want to do, isn't it? I just want to make you feel good, don't I?" I nod slowly and she mimics the movement.

Violet nods, cheeks flushed and eyes glassy. It's perfect. I have her in exactly the state I want her.

"So you're gonna let me do that now, aren't you?"

"That would be nice."

I lean in and suck her plush bottom lip between mine. "Want me to take you upstairs?"

"We can stay here," she murmurs.

"You sure? I want you to be comfortable."

"Granite can be comfortable."

I chuckle and kiss my way down Violet's neck.

Just as I'm about to shove my face in her cleavage, she asks, "Am I boring in bed?"

I lift my head to meet her gaze. "What?"

She bites her lip, looking uncertain. "Am I too . . . vanilla?"

"Vanilla?"

"Yes. Vanilla. Like plain, not exciting."

"You dress my dick up like a superhero. That's not vanilla, Violet."

"I think that's probably just weird. I mean, like, am I adventurous enough?"

"Does this have anything to do with those movies you and Charlene were watching? That soft-core porn stuff you keep telling me is romantic?"

"They're based on books. We were doing a comparative analysis for our book club."

"I think you just like watching that guy walk around shirtless and pantless."

"He's got nothing on you." She slides her hands under my shirt and runs her palms over my pecs. Her gaze shifts to mine, uncertainty lingering. "Am I, though?" At my confusion, she clarifies, "Adventurous enough in bed?"

I take her face in my hands. "You're perfect. You don't need to do anything differently."

"So you don't want to tie me up or gag me or anything?"

I have no idea how we went from butt lube to gagging and binding, but then Violet's brain is a weird place most of the time, and she and Charlene did have a movie marathon last week. "I guess if you *wanted* to be tied up we could try it, but I kinda like your hands on me, and a gag would make it difficult to hear you chant your love of my cock."

Violet breathes a relieved sigh and her palms slide down over my abs. "I like my hands on you, too, but the chanting is kind of beyond my control."

"I like you out of control and I love the chanting." I lean in for a kiss. Violet doesn't stop me, which is good, because I want to put my hard-on somewhere nice and wet and warm.

I keep it light on the tongue, which drives Violet insane—she really loves mouth fucking. It doesn't take long before her hands are in my hair and I'm lifting her to sit on the edge of the counter so she can wrap her legs around my waist. Pulling me in tight with her heels, she gets her dry hump on.

While she grinds her cotton-covered pussy on my bare cock, I get rid of her shirt and camisole. Before I remove the bra, I take a few seconds to nuzzle her rack. Violet has the best boobs in the world. They're soft, yet firm and the perfect handful, or mouthful, depending. She has the sweetest, most delicate nipples. They're perfect for licking and sucking and biting—but gently. I nibble the swell as I flick the clasp on the back and set them free.

Cupping them, I bury my face in the lush cleavage, while I thumb her nipples. Violet's knees press hard against my hips and her fingers anchor in my hair. She drags in a gasping breath as I draw one of those pert nipples into my mouth, flicking it with my tongue like I would her clit. She bucks against me, as if those two parts of her body are directly connected. I move to the other breast, repeating the same suck, lick, flick before I come back up to kiss her pretty lips.

Smoothing my hands down the sides of her neck, I inform her what my plan is, so she can tell me if she likes it or not.

"I'm going to get you naked now, and then I'm going to eat you for lunch. After that, I'd like to get inside you. Does that sound okay?"

"Oh, God. Please." I help her shimmy out of her shorts and panties and then I drop to my knees, kissing the insides of her thighs before I bury my face between her legs. She writhes against my mouth, telling me how much she loves my tongue and my fingers, and that she can't wait to give Super MC a big hug. I almost laugh at that part, but then her legs clamp around my head and I have to hold her thighs open so I can breathe through her orgasm.

Violet drops back on her elbows as I push up to a stand, swiping my mouth with the back of my hand. She knocks over the bottle of butt lube and it starts to roll away. Despite being a little orgasm uncoordinated, she nabs the bottle before it can get too far. She's still propped up on one elbow, legs spread wide, breasts heaving. She bites her lip and looks from me to the lube and back again. Then she glances at the butt plug a few inches from her knee, and back at the lube.

"So how does this stuff work exactly?"

I tell myself not to get excited, because this doesn't mean that she's asking me to use it on her. She's just curious. It's just a question. I clear my throat before I answer, so as not to sound like an excited pre-teen boy. "It's a muscle relaxer."

Her brow furrows. "You mean like that painkiller you get from Canada for your back, the one with Pinocchio on it?"

It takes me a second to understand the reference. "You mean Robaxacet?"

"Yeah, that package freaks me out." She flips the bottle over to inspect the label. "So this is like liquid Robaxacet for my bum?"

I can't *not* laugh. "Um, I guess?"

"So do you just, like, squirt it on there and wait? What exactly is it relaxing?"

I take the opportunity for the potential it has, and run my hands up her thighs. "You know, baby. This is probably one of those times where it might be better if I show you how it works, rather than tell you."

"Of course, you'd say that. Maybe I should be the one trying it on you, not the other way around."

I snort my disbelief. "You wanna stick your finger up my ass?"

Violet makes a face. "Ew. No. I like looking at your naked ass, and grabbing it, but I don't want to stick things in it the way you seem to want to stick things in mine. I want to rub it on your cock to see if makes you soft."

"It won't make me soft."

"How do you know?"

"Because that's not how it works."

Violet frowns and sits up, her eyes narrowed, legs still spread wide. She pokes me in the chest with one of her painted, pointy fingernails. "Have you invaded someone's Area 51 before?"

"What?"

"Butt sex! Have you had it before?"

I have to fight a smile, because she sounds awfully jealous despite her adamant stance on the subject—well, adamant until I get anywhere close to that area when I'm taking her from behind, then she gets all high-pitched and breathy. I don't answer right away on purpose. It's not nice of me, but her jealousy over something that's never happened is an ego stroke.

"Have you?"

I rub slow circles with my thumbs close to the juncture of

her thighs. "Would it upset you if I had?"

"Super MC is mine." She grabs hold of my cock and squeezes possessively. "Was it some slutty puck bunny who had a part-time job as an amateur porn star?"

"I haven't had anal sex, Violet, not with an ex-girlfriend and definitely not with a puck bunny. You know I wasn't into that scene before I met you." Although once I tried the anal route with an ex-girlfriend. I didn't get very far, even with the butt lube. I've learned a lot since then, but Violet needs none of this information.

"So how do you know this won't make you soft?"

"Let's just say research. Also, how would that even work if that's what happened?"

"Oh, right." Her expression floats somewhere between skeptical and curious. "So if you haven't Area 51'd before, why are you so interested in it now?"

I go with the response I think will get me the best outcome. "You're my wife. I want every part of you."

She gets that soft look in her eyes, but it disappears rather quickly, though. "You know, that would be a lot more romantic if you were talking about my heart and soul, not my butt."

"All I wanted to do was have sex on the kitchen counter, the regular kind. You're the one asking questions about lube." I step between her legs and let my cock bump against her—nice and close to her pussy, but not so close that there's contact with the good parts.

"Well, it's right here, and you're so excited just about the thought and the plug and the lube, and I know you want to get in there with Super MC, but that's not going to happen, because even though you try to deny it, he's huge." She's getting flail-y again.

I gently remove the lube from her hand and set it on the counter. Then I take her face between my palms and brush my lips over hers. "Relax, Violet. We've talked about this before. I'm well aware that getting a finger in there doesn't mean my cock is next."

"But you'd like it to be." I think she wants to come across as annoyed, but she just sounds breathless.

"I don't need to get anything in there. Ever again, if that's what you're worried about." I run my hands down her sides, skimming the curve of her breasts. "Are we done with this discussion? Should I take you upstairs and love you a little more before I have to meet with my agent, or should I just keep loving you here?"

"We can be done . . . for now." She threads her fingers through the hair at the nape of my neck. "And here is good."

She tugs me closer. Her boobs press against my chest and she wraps her legs around my waist again so we're flush against each other. I kiss her, all nice and soft and easy, fingertips skimming from her sides to her hips so I can pull her closer to the edge of the counter.

That's when Violet starts with the grind-and-moan, making all her sexy sounds, like she's looking for more than just the friction of my cock rubbing on her clit.

She breaks the kiss long enough to ask, "Wanna bend me over the island?"

I fight a triumphant smile. Sometimes Violet says no, but really, when it comes down to it, she'll end up asking for the thing she doesn't think she wants. It just needs to be on her terms. "Is that what you'd like me to do?"

She makes an affirmative noise and pushes on my chest. I step back, giving her enough room to slip off the counter. I stay close as she turns and bends over, wiggling her ass a little as she rests her elbows on the granite and looks over her shoulder.

I give her a low appreciative whistle as I run my palms down her back and over her ass. "I didn't think it was possible, but those yoga classes seem to have improved on perfection."

Violet smiles and blushes a little. "You think?"

I hum an affirmative. "This is one biteable ass, baby."

She giggles as I run my hands over her backside a few more times, then I close the distance between our bodies until my cock is resting along the divide. Violet sucks in a surprised breath. I wait for her to tense, which she does, as expected—but a second or two later she arches.

I release one hip and use my hand to guide my cock lower. I very purposefully avoid any Area 51 contact. It's reverse psychology with Violet. When I don't do the things she expects—the ones that make her all clench-y and skittish—then all of a sudden she starts intimating that's exactly what she wants.

I slide past her entrance—the one to door number one— and rub my cock over her clit a few times, then ease back so I tease her with the head. Violet glances over her shoulder, her lip caught between her teeth.

"What's up, baby? Am I taking it too slow?" I push in, but just the tip.

She makes one of her little moany, discontent sounds when I shift my hips back, and don't make a move to get inside any more than the first inch. The hand that isn't guiding my cock is strategically kneading her ass cheek. But I'm nowhere close to her No-Go Zone.

"Alex?"

"Mmm." I pause my torture and look up.

Her eyes dart from me across the counter to the bottle of lube. "Maybe, you . . ." She sucks in a breath when my thumb gets closer to the land of access-mostly-denied.

"Maybe I . . ." I let the words hang, waiting.

"Maybe you could demonstrate like you suggested." She slides a hand across the counter and pushes the little bottle a few inches closer to me. "So I know what it does, like you seem to."

I swallow a couple of times and surreptitiously clear my throat. Fuck yeah, this is going down. "You're sure?"

She nods and nudges it with the tip of her finger. It falls to its side and rolls toward me. I keep up the slow cockhead-to-clit rubbing while I open the bottle with my free hand. It's a lot of multitasking, but I can deal, especially if it means I get to go where I usually don't—even if it's only with digits.

Rubbing some liquid on my fingers, I'm forced to release my erection. I don't want to lose the contact completely, so I ease in a couple inches, enough that she can feel me, but not enough to really get her anywhere good.

And that's when I start with the controlled rubbing, just circling around and around door number two with my thumb, kneading her ass cheek with my free hand. I don't make any kind of move to get in there—I'm smarter than that. I know my wife. I know what gets her going. The key here is patience.

"Alex," she whimper-moans.

"Yeah, baby." I add the tiniest bit of pressure, then go back to circling, following with a shallow thrust and retreat—with my cock, not my thumb and the back door. I'm maybe halfway in and that's where I'm going to stay.

"You're teasing," she whines.

"Am I? You don't like this? Want me to stop?" It's

probably just as much torture for me as it is for her.

"Alex."

I pull out—all the way and she makes an angry noise. "Tell me what you want, baby."

She shoots an angry glare over her shoulder. "I know what you're doing."

"I'm giving you what you want, what you asked for, aren't I?" I move the thumb hovering over door number two out of range so she can't push back against it. "And right now, I'm just looking for clarification on what exactly that is, because I don't want to be sneaking things where they're not welcome."

She pushes up on her toes and reaches across the table. It takes three tries before she's able to snatch the plug and slide it across the counter. I block it before it can fall over the edge.

"What do you want me to do with this?"

She glares at me. "What do you think?" And then she mumbles, "Invade Area 51."

I'd like to make her repeat that, but I don't want to risk her taking away the toy, literally. "Are you sure?" My excitement is impossible to conceal, not in the way the words come out or the way my cock jerks.

"Just do it before I change my mind."

"If it's not good, tell me, okay?" I pour a little too much lube on it, making it extra slippery. It's actually probably no bigger than my thumb, which has staged an invasion before. It's like the training wheels of butt plugs—which sounds so wrong. But it's a start.

I may never get in there. I know that. Her concerns about my size are valid, but this is better than no access at all, ever. I tease her like I was doing before until Violet expresses her impatience. I trade my thumb for the tip of the plug and the real teasing commences.

It takes a good five minutes of cajoling, reassuring, and checking in on how she feels before I'm able to ease it all the way in. I get a lot of moaning, and several instances where she expresses her concern about anything bigger ever fitting in there. But every time I suggest stopping, she says no, loudly. And my view is absolutely motherfucking fantastic, so I'm happy for it to take as long as she damn well needs to get it in there.

When it finally is, I rest a palm on either ass cheek and exhale a deep sigh. "Invasion complete."

Violet cranes her neck, not that it's going to help her see what I can. "Really?"

I barely lift my gaze with my nod.

She reaches back and skims over the end of the plug with her red, white, and black nails. The index one is patterned with the team logo. "Wow, that doesn't feel bad at all." She presses on the end a bit and gasps. All of a sudden she pushes upright and spins around. Before I have a chance to react, she's running down the hall.

"Where're you going?" My confusion keeps me frozen for a couple of seconds before I chase after her.

She slips into the powder room and the light comes on. When I peek my head in, I find her with her back to the mirror, hands on her ass, spreading her cheeks as she tries to look over her shoulder.

"What're you doing?" The gravel and the pitchiness are pretty obvious.

"I just wanted to see what put that expression on your face."

"What expression?"

"The one where it looks like you're two seconds away from jizzing."

Fair enough. "Do you get it now?"

She lifts a shoulder. "I guess." Then she grazes the plug again, maybe just a little fascinated. Circling it, she gasps. "Okay. I think I get it."

My erection is pretty much throbbing at this point. So I cross the room in two strides and replace her exploring fingers with my own, tapping the plug a couple of times just to hear her sharp inhalation of breath. I slip my free hand between her legs, brushing over her clit before I slide a finger inside her. It's obviously tighter, thanks to the ass invasion.

Violet grabs my shoulders, her eyes wide, mouth dropping open on a quiet, "Oh."

"How's that feel?"

"I don't—oh, God—that's so—" She follows it with a moan, and some shoulder clawing.

"Should I stop?"

"No!" she shouts. "Just keep doing that thing with your fingers. Holy shit fuck." The chanting starts after that, and a minute later her face is mashed against my chest, a full body shudder rocking her slight frame. I'm fully responsible for holding her up, because she's gone lax against me.

Eventually, I begin to withdraw my fingers. She clamps her legs shut and looks up at me with wide, panicked eyes. "You better be replacing those with Super MC."

"I can do that. Definitely." She unclamps her legs and surveys the bathroom, possibly considering her options. Grabbing the edge of the vanity, she gives it a little shake, possibly to make sure it's secure since we haven't had sex in this bathroom. Although I'm fairly certain Ballistic and Lily have.

"Seems sturdy," she mumbles. Then she turns around and hoists herself up on the vanity. As soon as her ass touches the granite counter, she shrieks and hops off, her knees almost buckling.

"Forget about this?" I pat her ass.

"You could've stopped me." She wraps her arms around my neck and rubs herself on my chest, like a frisky cat.

"You want to go upstairs for this part? Maybe make use of our bed?"

"Um . . . it's far away, though."

"It's also softer."

I make the decision for us by lifting her up by the back of her legs, right under her ass, which forces her to wrap her legs around my waist and hold onto my shoulders. I'm careful—but quick—going up the stairs, and gentle when I lay her on the bed. I hold myself above her. "You want me to un-invade Area 51 first, or . . ."

"Um, no? Isn't the point that it stays put when you're getting beaver hugs?" She's understandably uncertain. "It'll stay where it is, won't it?"

"Yeah. It's not going anywhere." This is going to be way better than the times I've had a finger in there. "It'll be tight, though." My voice is shaking I'm so excited.

She arches a brow. "Isn't it always?"

"Tighter than usual." I lower my hips and slide my cock over her clit. "More than when I've used a finger."

"I think that's okay."

She sighs as I go lower and circle her slick entrance, bumping up against the plug as I tease her opening. She lifts a hand, fingertips skimming along the V. "Wait."

Fuck. I shouldn't have offered the bed—I should've just been selfish and took advantage of the situation and her orgasm acquiescence in the bathroom. I pause with the tip just barely in and lift my gaze to meet hers.

"Shouldn't we do this, like, doggy style?"

"Huh?"

She makes an attempt at sitting up, but her eyes widen a bit with the movement so she settles on her elbows. "Well, doesn't it defeat the whole purpose in this position? I mean, you've got this thing in my butt. Shouldn't you be able to see it while we're sexing? Otherwise, why's it even there?"

It's a valid argument. I'm probably not going to last very long if she's on all fours, but good fucking God, as long as I can make her come first, my longevity isn't important. "I, uh, I wanted to be able to see your face so I can gauge how it feels for you."

"You don't need to see this." She motions to her face. "Since when have I ever been quiet about how things feel?"

"That's a good point."

She flips over onto her stomach and pushes up so her ass is in the air. Jesus Christ. This is just perfectly obscene. Violet snaps her fingers. "Are you going to get on the bed with me, or are you just going to stand there and stare at my ass?"

"I'm coming."

"Hopefully not yet since you're not even in me. I better get an orgasm out of this, or it's never happening again."

I climb up behind her. "Is that a threat?"

"I'm just saying, if you want to add Area 51 invasions to the mix, then you better be bringing your 'A' game, Alex."

She's making it sound like this isn't going to be a one-time occurrence. "I'll bring it baby. I promise." I shift her around on the bed so I can see her reflection in the mirror across the room—that way I can read her facial expressions just as much as her body language and, of course, her personal sex soundtrack.

I take several long moments to appreciate the view before me. I'm a boob man, always have been, always will be, but Violet has a great ass. It's extra curvy these days thanks to all the yoga. I run my hands over her backside, then lean down to give the right cheek a little nibble. Violet gasps and then moans as I slip my fingers between her legs to caress her.

I use my fingers first, just to get her ready, and when the moans turn to demands, I get into position. I ease in slowly, watching the head disappear.

"Holy fuckballs." She holds up a hand as if she's tapping out of a fight.

I freeze. "Too much? Should I stop?"

"Yes. No. Don't stop."

"Are you sure?" I cross my fingers—literally, I cross them—and ease in maybe half an inch.

She drops her head and I push a little more. This time she slaps the comforter. "Wait."

I stop. I'm maybe halfway at best, probably more like a third. I have a lot more to go. It's so fucking tight. It reminds me of the first time we had sex, although I'm pretty sure this beats that in terms of snugness.

Violet lifts her head and cranes her neck, trying to look at me over her shoulder. "Holy hell. I can feel that. Like I can feel Super MC sort of pushing against it. Jesus, Alex. Do you feel that the way I do?"

I have to take a couple of deep breaths, because her verbalizing the sensations is making it very hard to focus. "Yeah," I croak. "I can feel it."

"That's unreal," she mumbles. Then she reaches back and slaps blindly at my thigh. "Keep going, but slow."

I slide in another inch, and then another. Violet holds her hand up, then drops it right away, so I keep going. I'm drunk on sensation. I can actually feel the moment I pass the end of the plug through that thin barrier, because the tightness eases around the head of my cock.

Violet's head shoots up and drops just as quickly. The words *Oh my God* are chanted several times as she kicks her feet against the comforter—almost like a temper tantrum but with moaning instead of screaming, although those might be next depending on how hard she comes. The kicking creates movement and puts pressure on the plug, which puts pressure on my cock.

"Baby? Are you okay? Do you need me to pull out? Do you need me to . . . uninvade your ass?" *Please say no.*

"No!" The word is muffled because her face is mashed into the comforter. She turns her head to the side and takes a gasping breath. "I'm gonna come, Alex. Probably the hardest I've ever come in my entire goddamn life, and if you stop, I will have orgasm deprivation rage."

"I won't stop. You want me to thrust?"

"Yes. So much thrust. Please give."

The words barely make sense, but I do as I'm told. Violet reaches between her legs as I find a slow, easy rhythm. The view combined with the sensation is unreal. I skim the plug with my thumb, then put a little pressure on it to see what happens.

Violet explodes. A string of profanity and some cock love chanting begins. I keep pumping, faster, but not harder, and less than ten strokes later, I'm gritting my teeth and pushing in deep. Violet screams my name, clawing at the bed, her entire body shaking violently before she goes limp, her face and chest press against the comforter, her ass still in the air.

I'm still inside her, in no rush to leave all the tight warmth behind. "Violet? Baby? You okay?"

She mumbles something.

"What?"

She blows her hair out of her face. "Just because I liked it doesn't mean Super MC is next."

I chuckle. "I know."

"And don't think just because I let you do this this one time you get to do this all the time."

"I know that, too." I ease out and roll her onto her side, then curl my body around hers.

"It's a special occasion thing."

"Okay." I kiss her shoulder and smile.

She turns in my arms and gives me a serious look. "No more than once a month."

I nod in somber agreement. "Definitely not more than that."

"More than that would be excessive."

I kiss the end of her nose. "You can make me an Area 51 Access Pass for those special occasions, if you want."

"Ohh! I could make Super MC a little FBI vest, like he's going on a mission!"

"If that's what you want to do, I won't stop you." I dip down to capture her lips. As if I'm going to tell her no. "Just remember Velcro only."

"I'll make it out of black liquorice so it's edible."

"Even better. Now stop talking so I can kiss you." I cover her mouth with mine.

"Wait." She pushes away, eyes wide. "Do you think if you accept that endorsement campaign they'll send you more butt stuff? Like the mountain of condoms they sent before?"

"It's possible."

"Huh. Well, that would save a lot of money in online purchases, wouldn't it?"

"I guess it could, if you were planning on making a lot of online purchases in the near future."

She plays with the hair at the nape of my neck. "Something to think about, anyway. What time do you have to leave for your meeting?"

I check the clock. "I have another half hour."

"Does Super MC want another beaver hug before you have to go?"

"He sure does." I tip her chin up so I can kiss her.

Score another one for Waters.

Violet might be crazy, but she's the perfect crazy for me, and there's no one in this world I would rather love.

NOTE TO READERS:

Alex isn't getting in there. Like seriously. This is as far as he's going to get. His dick is mammoth. It's a curse. Don't feel too sorry for him. He doesn't actually know what he's missing. Butt (hehe) I had so much fun writing this, so thanks for letting me share this crazy with all of you. Now you know Darren and Charlene are getting freaky. Just you wait for the conversations between Violet and Charlene. 2018, my friends.

Much love and gratitude for my amazing readers <3
Helena

WHY DID I WRITE this? Because Super MC. Does there really need to be another reason? Nope. Not at all.

Mrs. Waters,

    This Valentine's Day is extra special because it's the first one we get to celebrate with you as my wife. Can I tell you how much I love that? And you, of course. Wife is my new favorite word. Well, one of them. I'm also partial to the word boobs, specifically when in reference to you showing me yours, or wrapping your boobs in a new bra, or unwrapping. Anything having to do with your boobs makes me happy. I plan to enjoy them later tonight, along with the rest of you.

    You'll be picked up at eleven for an afternoon of pampering. Maybe, if it's not too much trouble, you can do that crystal thing like you did a while back? I really enjoyed that. A lot. Like so fucking much. I promise I'll make it worth your while if you do. I promise to do that anyway, but the sparkle makes it extra special.

    I thought about making a dinner reservation, but

then there's the whole sharing thing, and someone other than me having your attention, and you know how I feel about that, so I'm ordering in for us. I hope you're okay with that. All you have to do is show up. I bought you some new lingerie for tonight, too. And a few other fun things I can't wait to show you.

The Super MC wrote you a little poem, just something for you to think about while you're being pampered today.

Roses are red, Violets are blue,
So are my balls when I don't get to see you.
This Valentine's Day is your first as my wife,
The beaver with whom I'll spend the rest of my life.
To demonstrate my ever-growing love for you,
I wanted to try a little something new.
I know you're scared to let me in your Area 51,
But I think we both know we're well beyond Alex's thumb.

I had nothing to do with that poem. At all. My dick channeled that. In no way support or endorse Super MC's message.

I love you.
See you tonight.
I can feel you clenching from here.

XO Alex (Mr. Waters) and the Super MC

WHY DID I WRITE THIS? Last year our daughter got into corking, and well . . . I had some ideas that were not appropriate and decided to channel them into a super ridiculous outtake. The ™ is not real, but I thought it was hilarious.

"DO I EVEN WANT to know what this is about?" Charlene plunks down on the couch and motions to the spread before me.

"I'm trying to make those fingerless hand warmer things, but I suck at crocheting and knitting, so I thought this might work better." I hold up the corker. "I'm having issues with sizing and making a thumb hole, though." This is way harder than I expected it to be and I told the nice people at the soup kitchen that I'd have a dozen pairs of fingerless gloves for the holidays. So far all I have are a bunch of tubes in various sizes.

Charlene picks up a red tube and slides it on her finger. "Not sure you're having much success with the fingerless gloves."

"I'm sure there's a way to make this work."

"Vi, this is a finger warmer. No adult human could get this over their wrist." She gives me her super creepy wide-eyed doe look and says, in a horrible voice while wiggling her finger, "Redrum, redrum."

"Don't be an asshole!" I try to snatch it from her finger, but she's fast and more coordinated than I am, hiding it behind her back.

I pick up another tube. This one is bigger. I tried to get creative, it's red and black, and I made an attempt at putting Alex's number on it. It didn't work that well. It sort of looks like a four, but it also sort of looks like two stick people getting it on doggy style. Turns out, corking and sewing aren't quite the same thing. All I have to worry about with a sewing machine is not stitching up my finger. It's pretty foolproof since there's a guard and all. Corking doesn't allow for much inventiveness from what I've learned so far. Which admittedly isn't much.

I manage to get my hand through the tube. It's snug, but I still have no idea how I'm going to make a thumbhole without completely ruining it. "Oh my God! I have the best idea!"

"Let this be your one reminder that whenever you say that, something embarrassing usually happens."

"Whatever, Char. You're used to it."

She shrugs, because it's true.

"I'll be right back!" I leap off the couch, slam my shin into the coffee table, and fall on the floor, holding onto my knee while I rock back and forth, moaning in pain for a good minute—at least it feels that long. Charlene just sits on the couch, muttering *Redrum*, wiggling her finger at me.

Eventually, I limp my way upstairs and return a few minutes later with my collection of fake penises.

Charlene raises an eyebrow. "You know I love you, Vi, but Darren doesn't like to share and I really like dick."

"Ha-ha. Alex doesn't like to share either, and I obviously like dick, too." I motion to the pile of silicone penises. "Oh! I need one more thing!" I rush back up to my office, returning with the most important penis of all: the Play-Doh replica I made of Super MC the weekend Alex proposed to me. It also happened to be the weekend I almost decapitated his dick, but we don't talk about that, and I've learned a lot about penis costumes since then.

"I thought Alex made you get rid of the dick sculpture. Wasn't it starting to mold?" Charlene's nose wrinkles.

"I varnished it so it's fine now. And I keep it in my office so he doesn't throw it out." Sometimes, when Alex is away and I miss him, I just hold onto it or rub it. It's soothing. Also, it's like having a mannequin for when I make Super MC costumes.

I take the corked tube off my wrist and shimmy it over the head of the Super MC sculpture. It takes some work to get it on, and one of the googly eyes I glued onto the head pops off in the process, but once it's past the mushroom top, it slides on nicely.

I adjust it so only the head peeks out and Vanna White my new invention. "It's a Weiner Warmer™!"

Charlene picks up a slim vibrator and slides one of the tubes over it. "A dick cozy."

It's at this moment that the house alarm dings, signaling that my husband is home. "Oh shit!" I cradle my now one-eyed Super MC against my chest. Alex obviously doesn't know I haven't gotten rid of it. I can't hide it upstairs because he's coming down the hall, so I do the next best thing and tuck it carefully behind the couch cushion so as not to break it. The Play-Doh is tough, but still, I take no chances with my Super MC sculpture.

"Hey, baby, I'm home!" Alex calls out at the same moment he rounds the corner. Behind him is Darren, Charlene's boyfriend.

I was so busy worrying about the safety of the Super MC sculpture that I failed to consider the coffee table covered in my modest collection of pretend penises. Oh, and a butt plug, but I grabbed that by accident.

Alex's smile turns into a confused frown as he processes the scene before him. The table and couch are littered with plastic friends and yarn corked tubes in various colors and sizes. Charlene is currently holding my pink vibrator, a lime green tube covering its middle. It's a good color combination, actually. Purple would work, too.

"Uh, what the fuck is going on here?" Alex asks.

"I was trying to make fingerless gloves," I explain.

"That really doesn't explain why your entire vibrator collection is on our living room table."

"Huh." Darren's eyebrows lift.

Alex looks over his shoulder, frown still in place. "What?"

Darren shrugs and rubs his bottom lip. It looks like he's trying not to smile. He's also not looking at Alex. His gaze is fixed on Charlene. "Nothing."

Alex crosses his arms over his chest, cocks a brow, and waits for an explanation.

"I was corking."

He looks back and forth between Charlene and me, his expression incredulous.

I roll my eyes, pick up a corker, and throw it at him. Of course, he catches it no problem. If he'd thrown it at me, it likely would've hit me in the face. "Corking, c-o-r-k-i-n-g, not *porking*, you pervert. I thought I could make those fingerless glove things for the soup kitchen, but I never learned how to knit or crochet, so I went with corking, but all I can do is make tubes, and I can't figure out how to add a thumbhole, so I figured I could repurpose them—"

"—and turn them into dick cosies." Charlene holds up the pink vibrator wearing the green sheath as an example.

"Weiner Warmers™ sounds better," I argue.

"Whatever you call them, we're not bringing them to the soup kitchen, Vi."

"What? Why not?"

"Because there will be children and families there. We can't hand out dick warmers."

Dammit. He has a point. I throw my hands up in the air. "Well, I have to bring something and I'm running out of time. I could bake cookies or something."

"No!" all three of them yell at the same time.

"I'm getting better at baking," I mutter. I'm really not. I always burn them. Even with a convection oven.

"We can just buy gloves, " Alex says.

"Well, what am I going to do with all of these?" I flop back against the couch and gesture to the pile of Weiner Warmers™.

"I'll take one off your hands." Darren gives me one of his rare smiles. It's a disarming expression on him, likely because I don't see it often and it makes him look . . . almost sweet when he does. He picks up one of the girthier ones, slides three fingers into it, and scissors them around to test for stretchiness. Apparently satisfied, he shoves it into his pocket.

"Oh! I could give one to all the guys on the team! Jock strap cosies!"

"You are not giving all the guys on the team dick cosies."

"I'm not offering to put it on for them, Alex. I'm offering them something to protect their dicks from jock strap chafing. It's thoughtful."

"Still, no." His arms are crossed over his chest, forearms tight. Alex is a little territorial. Mostly I don't mind because he's also super sensitive and considerate.

I can also sort of see why he wouldn't want me to give his teammates Weiner Warmers™. But that doesn't mean I'm not going to do it anyway. At least with our close friends. Because when the hell have I ever been appropriate?

Fifteen minutes later, Alex is whispering into my ear to put all my fake penises away. Darren and Charlene are still here and we've ordered in from my favorite Italian restaurant, the one that uses lactose-free cheese on their chicken parm.

"They're my Weiner Warmer mannequins."

He gives me a look. It's not a happy one. I'm pretty sure this is because Darren is here, getting a look at all the things I put in my beaver when Alex isn't around to feed me his wood. And the one I let him put in my Area 51 on special occasions when he convinces me having a million orgasms in a row is a good idea.

"Fine, I'll put them away," I grumble.

I gather them all up and take them upstairs, dumping them onto the bed. I'll worry about putting them away later. Except the Area 51 invader. All it takes is a glimpse of that thing and Super MC tries to stage a revolt and burst through Alex's pants, so I usually tuck it in the back of the drawer.

Maybe that's why he was so intent on making me put them all away.

After dinner we play an exciting game of Scrabble. I end up with the *j* and the *z* at the same time. This would be terrible, except I also have one of the blank tiles and an *i*. I'm forced to put down three low point words, cutting my lead significantly. My patience pays off, though, because a triple word score comes up. I'm bouncing in my seat when I get to put the word *jizzy* down on the board.

Alex purses his lips. "Jizzy isn't a word, Violet."

He gets all English major uppity when we play Scrabble. It's entertaining.

"It's in the Urban Dictionary," I argue. I don't honestly know if this is true or not, but I have to assume it is.

His expression is smug, lip curling in a sneer as he challenges me. "Use it in context then."

"Charlene's chest gets all jizzy when Darren gives her a pearl necklace."

Darren turns his head and coughs while Charlene uses her middle finger to adjust the pearls around her neck.

I get sixty-nine points for that word, which is awesome for so many reasons. I also win the game. Alex comes in last, only because his priority is to make great words even if he has to sacrifice points. It's terrible strategy, but whatever.

Charlene and Darren—who have been giving each other looks all night, as they do—leave around ten. The Weiner Warmers™ are still in a pile on the coffee table.

"I wonder if I could get some fleece-lined spandex and make fingerless gloves out of that." I nab one of the Weiner Warmers™ and slip it on my finger as I flop down on the couch. It's too big, so I have to shove another finger in there to make it snug.

"We'll just go out and buy some." Alex sits down beside me, eyes on my fingers as I try to get a third one into the tube. It's a tight fit, but I manage to do it.

"That defeats the purpose. I wanted to make something, not buy something. The Weiner Warmers™ would've been awesome if there wasn't the whole family aspect."

Alex picks up one of the narrow tubes and tries to slide it on his thick finger.

"You should use it for its intended purpose."

Alex gives me a dark look. "My dick won't fit in this, Vi."

It barely fits on one finger. Of course, it wouldn't fit Super MC. "Let me see if I can find one that will." I search the pile of tubes, looking for one that will fit Alex's monster cock when it's soft. He's both a show-er and a grower. When he's not hard, his dick isn't terrifyingly large, but then it starts to inflate. It doesn't scare me like it used to when we had our one-night stand that turned into an actual relationship.

The one that will fit with absolute certainty is still on my Super MC Play-Doh sculpture, but that's meant for him when he's hard. I select three different sizes, then push the coffee table out of the way and edge between his legs.

His grin is all smug excitement as I unbuckle his belt, pop the button, and pull down the zipper. He lifts his hips and pushes both his boxers and jeans down until his cock pops free and thwacks him in the stomach.

"You already have a semi."

"You're kneeling between my legs and you're about to put your hands on my cock. Of course, I have a semi."

He makes a move to grip his still somewhat floppy erection and I swat at his hand. "Don't do that! I want to see if I have to make size adjustments, and I can't do that if you're already fully hard."

Alex quirks a brow, but drops his hands to his thighs. "Have at it then, baby."

The smallest of the three Alex-sized Weiner Warmers™ definitely won't fit right now, so I go with the next one up. His erection jerks when I place the tube over the head and start sliding it on. "Isn't it soft?"

"Yeah, super soft." Alex nods.

"I used the same kind of yarn Sunny likes for baby blankets."

"Oh yeah?" Alex licks his lips, fingers twitching on his thighs while I work my magic.

It's not super easy to get it over the head since it's the thickest part, but once it's past the ridge, it slides down real nice. I'd say Alex is about three quarters of the way hard by the time I'm done adjusting. It's a little long, and the head of his cock just peeks out, so I fold the top down so it looks like his snuffie is wearing a turtleneck.

"Doesn't he look awesome?" I smile up at Alex. "Oh! Hold on!" I use his knees to push to a stand.

"Where are you going?" His voice is a little high and pitchy.

"I'll be right back!" I call over my shoulder as I dash out of the room.

I find my baking supplies, along with some clear and black icing, and rush back to where Alex is still sitting. Super MC stands tall and proud, wearing a Weiner Warmer. This one is black with a stripe of gray around the neckline. I kind of want to put a tie on him so he looks like he's wearing a suit.

When he sees what's in my hands, his eyes narrow. "What the hell is that for?"

"I want to put eyes on him."

"No."

"Come on, Alex." I motion Super MC, who looks like he's wearing a super cozy sweater. "He's adorable. Just let me put a face on him and take a picture, please?"

Alex's expression changes from unimpressed to downright horrified. "My dick is not fucking adorable." He makes a jabby motion with his hand toward his crotch. "He's formidable."

"I could give him an angry face if you want."

"No face."

Now Alex says this, but he's not moving from his spot on the couch, and he hasn't attempted to remove the Weiner Warmer, so I think I'll probably be able to get what I want as long as I promise him something really good in return.

"If you let me put a face on him, I'll lick it off." I sink down between his knees.

His eyes light up just a bit, but his brow quickly returns to its furrowed state. "I want you to suck it off."

"Yay!" I wrap my hand around his covered penis and give the tip an affectionate kiss before I rub it on my cheek. "This is going to be awesome."

Alex groans, maybe in agreement, maybe because he's fully hard and the Weiner Warmer is stretched around the shaft. It might be tricky to get it over the head, but I'm sure it won't be too much trouble.

I unpack my penis decorating kit and get to work. I have to blot the top because Alex is already excited and he's leaking a little. I use the clear icing glue to place the eyes, checking a couple of times to make sure they're not wonky. Then I use a candy marker to draw on angry eyebrows. I have to blot the tip a few more times, because Alex is clearly excited about the part where I suck the face off and I have to redo the mouth twice because his dick twitches when I use the black icing to drawn a scowl, but when I'm done, his penis looks adorably formidable.

"Tada!" I do jazz hands and almost smack myself in the face. "Isn't he awesome?"

"Sure is. Now you can suck him off."

It doesn't escape me that Alex sometimes refers to his own penis as if it's another person. "I just need a picture first."

"Oh fuck no. You're not taking a picture."

"But you said I could."

"No. I said you could put a face on him and suck it off. At no point did I agree to photographic evidence."

Now it's my turn to frown. Actually, I pull out my pout. "But look at all the trouble I went to." I motion to his dressed up penis and gently stroke around the ridge. It kicks in my hand.

I think maybe I have him, but his expression flattens. "Still no."

Goddammit. I want a picture. This is just too awesome to go undocumented. I rack my brain for potential enticements. It takes me all of five seconds to come up with the one that will most definitely get me what I want. Which is a picture of Alex's penis dressed up in a Weiner Warmer wearing a very Scrooge-like expression. I need to learn how to knit so I can make it an ugly sweater.

"What if I gave you Area 51 access?"

Alex's eyes go wide and his erection kicks in my hand. "Dick access?"

I give him my *get real* face. "No, Alex."

His face falls for half a second before it lights up again. "With that plug from the endorsement?"

"Or the one Charlene gave me for my bachelorette party. Whatever you like more." For sure he'll pick the endorsement one, since it has the team logo emblazoned hologram style in the flared base. "I'll even let you do the double duty thing where you invade Area 51 and sex me from behind at the same time." The last time he did that I came like my beaver button was the source of the apocalypse. But I let him think I'm being generous and accommodating by giving him access to places I normally wouldn't.

He nods vigorously. "Okay." His hands smooth up and down his thighs. "Where's your phone?"

I reach behind me, snatching it off the coffee table, and snap a bunch of pictures before Alex can change his mind. I probably take a hundred in less than a minute. Alex is antsy and excited, so he has a hard time keeping his knee still.

Once I'm done with the mini photo shoot, Alex motions to the head of his cock. "Time to get rid of the face, baby."

Normally, when I do something like this, I'll take my time, but Alex seems to be in a bit of a rush, probably because of the Area 51 access I've granted him. I suck off each little candy eye and lick around the head to get most of the candy glue and the icing facial features. I wrap my lips around the head and apply some suction.

As soon as I pop off, Alex starts pulling on the Weiner Warmer. "Let's get this off and get upstairs." All he succeeds in doing is pushing it up where it gets stuck at the ridge.

"Let me help with that." It's a lot tighter now on account of Alex's excitement.

I have to smooth it back out. The easiest way to get this off would be to snip one of the stitches to give it a little more wiggle room, but I don't think Alex will ever let me bring a pair of scissors near his dick again, so that's out.

As soon I get the Weiner Warmer over the head, I make an attempt to do the whole sucking thing again, but Alex isn't having it. He picks me up, rushing the stairs to get to the bedroom. "This is going to be so fucking awesome."

And it is totally fucking awesome, especially since I get to come three times before Alex is even inside me.

NOTE: I know you are all worried about the Play-Doh dick sculpture. It's okay. Violet manages to get it back to her office in her secret hiding place without Alex finding out she still has it.

WHY DID I WRITE THIS? I wrote this piece for KU Korner's storytime a couple of years back and felt like this outtakes book was the perfect place to put it.

I LOVE SUMMER. SUMMER means lighter training schedules, vacations, and lots of time spent by the pool. And that means Violet in a bikini. I fucking love Violet in a bikini. I love her out of one, too, but there's just something about those tiny triangles of fabric, wet and clinging to my favorite parts of her body.

It's Tuesday, which means she's working from home, and the weather is gorgeous—warm but not too hot, and sunny with a light breeze. There's a reasonably good chance that she'll be outside, working by the pool. In a bikini. Hence my excellent mood post-hockey practice.

I pull into the garage and head inside, dropping my sweaty gym stuff in the laundry room. I nab a pair of clean swim shorts from the basket that has yet to be put away.

Even if she isn't already by the pool, I'm hoping my attire will inspire her to take a dip with me. And then we can have post-pool sex. Or in the pool sex depending on whether there are neighbors around. Violet's not very quiet during sex and the pool tends to be echo-y.

As I approach the French door leading to the backyard patio and Olympic-sized swimming pool, my favorite sight greets me—well, second favorite. Violet is indeed working outside. She's reclined in a lounger, her laptop set up on the side table, along with a pile of papers, holding an iPad.

She's wearing one of my favorite bathing suits. It's red with my team logo on the boobs and another one right over her crotch. It says *WATERS* on the ass, indicating it's mine. And that ass certainly belongs to me. Well, it belongs to Violet, but sometimes she lets me get a finger in there, and recently there was an incident with a butt plug that gives me some hope for more, one day, maybe.

I'm already tenting my shorts just thinking about getting her wet, and then naked. As I watch her through the window, I note just how ample her boobs are. They look . . . bigger somehow. There's more side boob than usual, and the cleavage is more . . . cleaveage-y. Maybe it's the angle of her chair, but they really do look larger. It's possible the window is distorting them.

I open the door, intent to find out if I'm right or if I'm just so amped up and horny that I'm imagining things. Violet looks up from her laptop and smiles. Her eyebrows pop up as her gaze moves down my body. "Hey sexy, you and Super MC look happy to see me."

I pat my barely contained cock as I saunter on over. "We sure are. You want to take a break and go for a little dip?"

She sets the iPad on top of the stack of papers and pushes

up out of the chair. "I'm pretty sure you're not going to leave me alone until I say yes." She gestures to my crotch. "Plus, that needs to be taken care of."

She adjusts the cups of her bikini, frowning as she tries to cover the side boob, only to make the cleavage situation worse, or better, actually. Her tummy is normally flat and toned thanks to the hours of yoga my sister forces on her, but today there's a little bump. Not much of one, but I notice it mostly because I spend a lot of time looking at my wife's incredible body in little to no clothing.

She throws her arms around my neck, her boobs squish against my chest, and she rises up on her toes, pulling me down so she can kiss me. She tastes like orange juice, another one of my favorite things.

"I love Tuesday lunch breaks," I mumble around her tongue. Sliding my hands down her sides, I cup her ass and pull her in tight against my erection.

"Super MC loves them more apparently." She tries to wriggle away, but I kiss a path along her neck and slide my hands down the back of her bathing suit, kneading her ass.

"There's no Area 51 access today, so you can stop while you're ahead." Violet pushes on my chest again. When I let her go, she steps around and dives into the pool. It's not terribly graceful, and there's a lot of splash, but she no longer belly flops every time, so that's an improvement.

She doggy paddles the rest of the way to the other side. I dive in and reach the edge at the same time she does. Reaching around, I cup her boobs in my palms. Based on the way they spill out of my palms, they are definitely bigger.

Turning her around, I move her closer to the shallow end so I can pin her against the side and we make out. When she starts up with the noises and the little hums, I begin to question whether or not it's a good idea to have pool sex if she's pregnant. Which she very well may be with her extra booby boobs. And she's been sleeping in a lot. Violet can always sleep in, but she's been hitting the snooze button more than usual. And last week she complained about nausea.

Is pool sex dangerous? Could the bromine harm the baby? Are we having a baby? I lift her up, setting her on the edge of the pool, and fit myself between her legs. My face is at boob level. They really are spectacular today.

"Maybe we should continue this inside."

"Why? No one can see us and I love pool sex. It's fun trying to be quiet."

"I don't know if it's safe."

Violet seems genuinely confused. "Why wouldn't it be safe? I promise not to chant about cock love this time."

"I'm not worried about the chanting." Although that is something to consider.

"So I don't get the safety issue."

I shrug. Maybe it is safe, but I can't be sure without looking it up on Google. I circle her navel with a fingertip and try a different approach. "Do you have some news you'd like to share?"

"What the hell are you talking about? One second we're making out and now you're worried about pool sex safety and asking me about news? Did you eat one of your dad's cookies or something?"

"No, I didn't eat one of my dad's cookies." My father tests strains of medical marijuana. It's an actual job, taxable by the government. "Are you pregnant?"

"What?" It's more of a screech than a word. She swats my arm.

"Are you insane? Why the hell would you think I'm pregnant?"

"Your boobs are bigger and there's a bump." I lean in and give her tummy a kiss. She's going to look so good pregnant. Her boobs are going to be the best. It's even okay that I won't be able to really love them the way I want to because they'll just look so fantastic.

"My boobs are bigger because I'm getting my period, and I'm bloated because I was craving ice cream, but thanks a lot for pointing out my bloatation bulge and assuming it's because you got me knocked up."

"It's not knocking you up if we're married. Are you sure you're getting your period? Maybe the ice cream is a pregnancy craving. You should take a test."

Now she just looks annoyed. "I'm not pregnant, Alex."

"How can you be sure? Isn't there a leftover pregnancy test from the time in the winter when you couldn't remember if you took your pill after the New Year's party?"

"There's probably fifty left over since you bought the econo box from Costco."

"Great, so you can use one." I look up at her expectantly. While I wait, I give her boobs a nuzzle.

Violet sighs. "We're not having pool sex until you have an answer, are we?"

I shake my head against her cleavage.

She pushes my face away. "Fine. I'll go pee on a stick, but I'm not pregnant."

I follow her into the house and try to trail her into the bathroom, but she won't let me come in. Less than a minute later, she opens the door and hands me the stick. "We have to wait two minutes. A plus sign means it's positive. No plus sign means I'm bloated with an ice cream baby."

I follow her to the kitchen, holding the stick, watching the two windows, waiting for the magic sign to appear. I check my phone six times in the following one hundred and twenty seconds. There's no plus sign.

"Maybe it's defective. You should take another one."

Violet gives me her annoyed face. "I'm not pregnant, Alex. I'm just bloated. Why do you look so disappointed?"

"I honestly thought you were pregnant."

"You're just looking forward to my boobs being huge."

"That's untrue." I wrap my arms around her and pull her against me. "I love your boobs just the way they are." Bending, I kiss each swell, then come up to give her lips the same attention. "Maybe you should think about going off the pill."

Violet takes my face between her palms so she can meet my gaze with a shocked one of her own. "Are you serious?"

I pull the tie around her neck and the one below her shoulder blades. "Just something to consider. We can do all kinds of practicing until you're ready."

"I love practice."

"Me, too." I rid her of her bottoms and set her on the island, fitting myself between her thighs as my swim shorts drop to the floor. "So we should start practicing right now."

NOTE: A LOT of people were super disappointed that she wasn't preggers. You guys are a bunch of loons, but don't worry. I remedy that issue, see PUCKED LOVE for details and keep reading for more details.

PRETTY EYES

Alex

WHY DID I WRITE THIS? Forever, who published THE GOOD LUCK CHARM suggested I write a little piece that included Ethan and the gang from PUCKED since I made him a trade from Chicago. I had a great time putting him in this super awkward scenario with his former captain and teammates wife ;)

I DROP DOWN ON the cedar bench and roll my neck, loosening up the kinks after my workout. Off-season is coming to an end, and that means training starts soon, and my lax schedule is about to change. Randy's sitting across from me, a towel draped over his lap. Lance is on his left and Rookie is on his right. Rookie isn't really a rookie anymore, but the nickname isn't going anywhere.

Darren takes up the space beside me, and next to him is Miller, who pats his stomach. "I ate too many wings last night."

"Looks more like you're the preggers one instead

of Sunny, aye?" Lance jokes, his Scottish accent more pronounced than normal.

Miller flips him the bird. "Eat a dick. I'm bloated."

"I only eat Poppy." Lance grins. "And yer bloated, my ass. Yer gonna need to do some serious sprints at training camp if yer wantin' to get rid of your dad bod before the season starts."

Miller looks down at his stomach and frowns. "It's not that bad."

Randy looks up from his phone to add his two cents. "You two sound like teenage girls after gym class. What's next, a vagina-waxing session?"

Rookie snorts beside him, but keeps his mouth shut otherwise.

"We should have a preseason barbecue or something, celebrate the end of summer, eh?" I suggest.

"That's pretty much every weekend at your place, isn't it?" Randy asks.

"I was thinking I might invite the whole team this time, kind of a good way to bring in the new season since we're going in without The Cup this year." Only making the first round of playoffs last season was a blow after the past few years, so I want to find a way to boost team morale.

"That's a good idea. Welcoming the new guys to the team off the ice is smart," Darren agrees.

Rookie laces his hands behind his head and looks over to Lance. "Too bad you're not still throwing parties, Romance."

"Pretty sure Poppy would hand him his balls on a platter if he was still inviting the bunnies over." Randy rubs a palm over his beard.

"Pretty fucking sure my girl would make donuts out of them if I pulled that shit." Lance shifts around, as if the image in his head makes him uncomfortable. "You're welcome to invite all the bunnies to yer place anytime, Rookie. Just don't be surprised if we take a pass on that party." He motions to the rest of us. "Since we'd all like to keep our balls."

"And I'm not a fan of sleeping in the spare room," Miller adds.

"Calm your tits, guys. It was a joke." Rookie makes a simmer down gesture. "My bunny days are over. I'm just saying, if anyone's got a sister, or a cute cousin they want to introduce me to—"

Randy swats Rookie with his towel. "Dude. No."

"What? Miller's married to Alex's sister, and Alex is married to Miller's sister," Rookie points out.

"Yeah, and you weren't here to see these two trying to break each other's noses every time one of them so much as breathed the wrong way. You keep your dick away from our relatives and you won't risk losing it," Randy replies.

"He's only saying that because he has a younger sister," Darren says with a wry smile.

"Really?" Rookie perks right now. "I didn't know you had a sister."

"There's a reason for that," Randy mutters. "She lives in Australia, so it's pretty unlikely you'll meet her. Ever."

"Oh." Rookie turns back to me. "So when's this party gonna happen?"

"This weekend, maybe? That should be enough time to throw something together."

"Don't you think you should check with Violet first?" Miller arches a blond eyebrow.

I wave him off. "I'm sure she'll be fine with it. We always have people over on the weekend."

"Yeah, but usually it's just us, not the whole team. Don't you remember what happened the last time you threw a big party?" Miller taps his knee and gives me a meaningful look.

"What happened last time?" Rookie asks.

"Nothing." I turn back to Miller. "There won't be Jell-O shooters this time. Or a vodka watermelon."

"You still might want to ask before you go inviting the entire team over is all I'm sayin'," he mutters.

"It'll be fine. We'll plan it for Saturday afternoon. It's supposed to be nice out."

Violet stands in the middle of the kitchen with her hands on her hips. She does not look impressed. Her boobs, however, look fantastic in the bikini top she's wearing. I love it when she works from home and uses the opportunity to get a little sun at the same time. "The whole team, Alex?"

I drag my gaze back up to her face and give her my best, reassuring smile. "It'll be great for morale and it's a good way to get to know the newer players. It'll help make them feel like they're part of something awesome. You won't have to do anything. I've got everything covered. I'm already on food and booze. All you have to do is wear a bathing suit and have a good time." I motion to her current attire. Well, mostly I motion to her boobs.

"You're already on food and booze?"

She doesn't seem the least bit swayed by my positive morale for the team spiel based on how incredulous she seems. Also, this is the second time she's repeated the things I say back to me. I'm taking this as a bad sign. "I'll take care of everything, baby. You don't have to worry about a thing."

She scratches her arm and the back of her neck, another bad sign. Violet gets stress hives, and the last thing I want is my wife covered in itchy, angry red welts. "It's not the party planning I'm worried about."

I come around the island and run my hands down her arms, but she brushes me off, stalks over to the fridge, and yanks open the freezer door. "Baby, come on. What are you worried about?"

Despite her issues with dairy, she pulls out a tub of ice cream. "What am I worried about?"

"Okay, this is the third time you've repeated my words back to me like I'm an idiot. Can you just tell me what the problem is so I can fix it?"

Violet throws her hands in the air. "I'm the problem!"

I put on my *what are you talking about* face, because I have a feeling I know exactly what the issue is and that maybe Miller was right. "What'd you mean?"

She yanks open the drawer and pulls out a spoon and waves it around in a slightly manic way. "Uh, do you remember what happened the last time you threw a party here? Because I sure do. Sort of. Thanks to the videos Charlene took, I have actual evidence of how ridiculously out of hand things got."

"Baby, you didn't know the watermelon was spiked."

"That doesn't change the fact that I sang 'I Like Big Dicks' at the top of my lungs or that I tried to twerk."

It was probably one of the funniest things I've seen her attempt. Violet is incredibly smart and flexible thanks to all the yoga she does with my sister, but she is not very coordinated outside of the bedroom. Not that I'd ever tell her that. "You were adorable."

"I was an asshole." She peels the cover off the ice cream. "Look." She motions to the tub as she digs her spoon in. "You're forcing me to seek solace in ice cream just by talking about this." She shoves the entire huge spoonful into her mouth, possibly to make a point.

I run a soothing hand down her arm. "I don't want to stress you out. I can talk to Lance or Randy, and see if they wouldn't mind hosting instead."

Violet makes a cringy face and rushes to the sink. She spits out the mouthful of ice cream and turns the water on, rubbing her temples. "Dammit, I have brain freeze from that." She drops the spoon into the sink and turns around with a sigh. "You can't have one of the other guys host."

"Sure I can. Lance won't have a problem with it."

"Yeah, but you're the team captain. Obviously, you need to be the host. I just don't want to do something embarrassing."

"Nothing you do embarrasses me, Violet." And I mean that truthfully. I love all of Violet's quirks.

"Everything I do embarrasses *me*, though." She blows out a long breath. "Can we confiscate everyone's phone as soon as they enter the premises? Like, can you for sure, *for sure*, guarantee that no one is going to record me doing anything dumb and post it on YouTube five years from now in retaliation for something you said that they didn't like?"

"YouTube probably won't even be a thing in five years."

Violet gives me the look. It's the one that tells me I'm treading on thin ice and the boobs may be off limits if I keep it up. I wrap my arms around her waist and pull her against me. "Listen, baby, these are my teammates. They know better than to take drunken videos of my wife and post them anywhere unless they want to eat their teeth. You have nothing to worry about. I promise."

Violet runs her hands over my chest, so, of course, I flex my pecs for her. She tips her chin up, still frowning a little, but I can see the moment she caves. "Fine. But no bunnies. You make sure those newbies know they can't just disappear behind the pool house to get a damn blowie."

I suppress a smirk. "It's not the newbies I'd be worried about there."

Violet purses her lips and wrinkles her nose. "I have no control over Randy and Lily. And Lily isn't a bunny, and they usually do that in bathrooms. It was only that one time behind the pool house."

"That you know of."

"Do you know something I don't?"

"No. I'm just saying with Randy and Lily, it's pretty likely it's happened more than once considering they disappear every five minutes to get each other off. Okay, I need to stop talking about this. Lily's like family and it grosses me right the hell out. I'll make sure the guys know that this is a bunny-free zone, but some of them might bring dates."

"Just make sure they're non-bunny dates."

"I'll do my best." I nuzzle into her neck. Now that my wife is on board with the plan, I need to do something to shift her focus. "Wanna get out the Fruit Roll-Ups and play dress up?"

Violet pushes back, eyes bright with excitement. If I know how to do anything other than shoot a puck, it's how to distract my wife. "Really?"

"As long as you have the mixed berry ones, I'll let you do whatever you want."

Violet jumps up and down, clapping excitedly. "Oh my God! Yes! I have those." She cups me through my pants and bends down until her face is at crotch level. "We're going to have so much fun."

Violet

"We are not making Jell-O shooters for this party." Since I'm not pregnant I can tie one on, but I'd like to attempt to keep it together for this party and Jell-O shooters make that difficult. I attempt to prevent Charlene from dumping six boxes of Jell-O powder into the grocery cart, but she starts girl slapping me in the middle of the aisle, which draws attention, so I'm forced to back off.

"Look, Vi, I know you're worried it's going to be like last time, but Jell-O shooters are light on the booze. I promise you'll be fine."

"But they're so delicious, and once I start eating them, I really can't stop, and the next thing you know, I'll have polished off a whole tray on my own and the nightmare will begin."

"I won't let you eat a whole tray." Charlene throws a tub of Cool Whip in. "Oh, and I can make flash cards with all the players, their number, and their name for you. We can go over them while we make shooters."

"Oh my God! Why didn't I think of that? There are just so many names to remember, and they always know who the hell I am, but I can only remember last names and their jersey number. I always blank out on first names. It's one thing when it's a few of the guys, but this is the whole team. I know I'm going to screw someone's name up. Remember when I mispronounced Kuntz?"

"Anyone could've made that mistake. Look at my last name? No one ever remembers the *H* is silent in Hoar." Charlene gives my shoulder a reassuring pat. "You're a lot better with people than you think you are."

"I'm really not," I mutter. "Can we stop in the ice cream aisle?"

"Only if we're picking up non-dairy frozen treats. You're not eating a pint of Ben and Jerry's four hours before people show up. You'll bloat like a puffer fish and then you'll refuse to go swimming."

I sigh despondently. "I'll get sherbet or gelato."

I don't actually have time to indulge in anything I shouldn't, because by the time we return from our shopping trip, it's already noon and guests will be arriving in two hours, which means Charlene and I have enough time to make rainbow Jell-O shooters but not much else.

Shots are always a bad idea, and yet we make these every single time we have a party. It's dumb. But there you go. While we mix Jell-O and vodka, Charlene flashes team faces at me. After the third time through, I manage to get all but a few names right. I'm pretty decent at memorization, and I'll at least be able to retain the information until I'm drunk, so I'm feeling a little better about things. Also, Charlene and I started drinking mimosas, so that helps, too.

As I'm going through them one last time, Charlene bends

down and retrieves a card from the floor. "I must've dropped this one."

She tosses it my way and I glance at the name and number. "Ethan Kase, forward, number forty-four." I flip the card over and am met with some stellar hotness. "Holy shit, check this guy out." I hold up the card facing Charlene.

"Oh yeah, he's not hard to look at, is he? And those eyes, my God, I bet panties drop as soon as he walks in the room."

"I wonder if he wears contacts."

"What're you girls talking about?" Alex comes up behind me and wraps an arm around my waist.

"How pretty this guy's eyes are."

Alex grabs the card from me and frowns. "Why do you have a picture of Ethan Kase?"

"I made team flash cards so Violet can put faces to names since we're usually looking at the back of a jersey," Charlene says.

"Huh, I guess that's a good idea. But Ethan isn't playing for Chicago anymore. He just got signed by Minnesota."

"So he's not coming then?" Charlene asks.

"No, he is. He's saying goodbye before he takes off."

"But wouldn't it be weird for him—" Charlene starts.

"Is this his real eye color?" I ask, interrupting their conversation with more important questions.

Alex shrugs. "I dunno. I don't spend much time staring into my teammates eyes. Why?"

"They're pretty, that's all." I take the card and shuffle it back into the deck.

The doorbell rings, and Alex steps away from me. "I'll get it." He pats me on the butt and grumbles something about his eyes being pretty too as he rushes to get the door.

"I think someone's jealous," Charlene whispers.

"Because I think some guy's eyes are pretty?" I roll my eyes. "Alex has a pretty dick, especially when it's dressed up like a superhero, and that's way better than having pretty eyes."

We both snicker and go back to making rainbow Jell-O shooters.

As promised, he's totally on top of things, with the planning and the taking care of everything, including me. I'm still nervous about embarrassing myself somehow today in front of all of his teammates. It's not as if I haven't done it before, but I would prefer not to have it happen every time we have some kind of party. A significant percentage of them have seen my bra, or heard me in the midst of an orgasm.

The new guys have only heard the stories—they don't have the memories—so it would be great if I could avoid doing something that will tarnish my already less-than-stellar reputation in their eyes.

I'm relieved that the first people to arrive are our friends. Sunny and Miller and Lily and Randy are followed by Lance and Poppy. Darren is somewhere around here. He floats in and out of the kitchen like a specter, pausing to whisper something to Charlene before he ghosts out again and does whatever Darren does. Presumably he's helping Alex set up.

Once the rest of my girl gang arrives, I feel a lot better. They're like a human safety net. They protect me from my own stupidity, or at least they try to. I wonder if they have a dog for that, kind of like a personal support dog, but this one would be a personal stupidity dog, to keep me from doing stupid things. I should look into it.

A few hours into the party everything seems to be going smoothly. I've done pretty well with remembering the players' names, so the flash cards can be considered a success.

Alex has set up a Ping-Pong table in the backyard and people are hanging out in the pool playing volleyball. Since the only balls I like to handle are Alex's, I sit on the sidelines and nurse mojitos with Charlene. Okay, maybe *nurse* is the wrong word. I'm on my third. I blame it on how hot it is and how delicious they are.

I survey the pool as Charlene and I take a seat at the edge so we can dip our feet in the water but stay out of the action. "You know, maybe I don't mind these team parties."

"I told you it wouldn't be like last time."

"And the view sure isn't bad. I mean, just look at that." I motion to the back of the guy launching himself into the air, water sluicing over his flexing muscles as he slaps the ball over the net. "It's the best back porn ever."

"Right?" Charlene nods her agreement while chewing on her straw. "So many nice bodies to ogle."

I clink my tumbler against Char's. "Amen to that, sister."

Poppy drops down beside me. She's wearing a huge hat and a pale green beach cover-up. Poor thing burns in minutes, especially on a day like today. "Enjoying the view?" she asks with a cheeky smile.

"Immensely." I take another sip of my drink, but end up slurping loudly. "Hmm. That went down a lot faster than I expected." I shake my empty tumbler, making the ice cubes rattle inside. "I should probably have a spacer before I refill, eh?"

"What is it?" Poppy asks.

"A mojito."

"Oh! I had one of those. They're pretty strong. Want me to get you a bottle of water?" Poppy offers. She's so freaking sweet.

"I need to use the bathroom anyway. Either of you want a bottle of water?"

Both Poppy and Charlene say yes. I feel pretty good about being responsible and not getting super shitfaced this early in the day. As I stand up, I realize I may actually be a little drunker than I originally thought, based on the way I wobble.

"You okay?" Poppy asks.

"Oh, yeah. You know me, walking in a straight line is tough on a good day, let alone when I've had a couple of mojitos."

Charlene snorts and gives me one of her half-drunk smiles. "Truth."

"Watch out!" someone yells, startling the three of us.

I look up in time to see a volleyball coming at me.

Now here's the thing about me. I'm a lot of things, but adept at catching things being thrown at me, on purpose or not, is not my strong suit. My first inclination is always to run away or duck. Except in this case I'm standing at the edge of the pool, so instead of being smart and taking a step back, I take a step forward.

The volleyball slams right into my boob as I tumble into the water. I shout my surprise and pain, because a hard ball to the tit hurts like hell, and I end up sucking in water.

A pair of hands settle on my waist and I'm pulled to the surface, sputtering and coughing. I grab on to a set of thick shoulders while I hack up half a lung.

"Shit. I'm so fucking sorry. Are you okay?"

I realize that the shoulders I'm holding belong to the male voice asking me a question, and that the male voice does not belong to my husband. However, I'm still trying to figure out how to breathe again, and my boob really hurts, so I keep one hand on his shoulder so he can continue to be my personal floatation device and wipe my hair out of my eyes.

Which is the moment I come face to face with the hot guy from the flash cards. Ethan Kase. I guess I am good at memorizing things even when I'm drunk. I cough at his chest a couple more times and get caught up staring at his eyes. They're just, so . . . odd. But cool, but odd. It's like the sun is trying to burst out of his right iris.

Let me preface what comes out of my mouth next, because I'm more than half in the bag. Also, I just fell into the pool and nearly choked to death, and I got hit in the boob, so my brain and my words are not in the same zip code. "Ooooohhhh, you have pretty eyes." I'm super close to his face, so I can see that he does not, in fact, wear contacts. I cough in his face again. And, of course, I feel bad, so I drag a wet hand over his chin. "Sorry 'bout that."

"Vi, baby? What's going on here?" Alex's voice comes from behind us.

Ethan's eyes go wide. "Oh shit, your Waters' wife? I'm so fucking sorry." He lets go of me and raises his hands in the air. "I am so sorry, Waters. I didn't mean to . . . I missed the ball."

I turn to see Alex standing at the edge of the pool. He looks pissed off. Although, I'm not exactly sure why. It's not like it's this guy's fault that I'm chronically clumsy and fell into the pool.

I doggy paddle back to the edge, still coughing a little, and accidentally kick Pretty Eyes. Yes, my brain starts to refer to him as Pretty Eyes instead of his name. Maybe those mojitos are a lot stronger than I thought. He mutters a curse and I look over my shoulder to find him cupping his man jewels. Of course, I have to kick the poor guy in the balls.

Alex reaches in and hoists me out of the water, still

glaring at Pretty Eyes.

"It was an accident," I cough. "Pretty Eyes was saving me from drowning because I'm clumsy."

Alex frowns. "Pretty Eyes?" Shitballs, he noticed my slip.

"Everything okay, Alex? The ball went high and hit Violet. Kase tried to stop it!" Randy calls from the other end of the pool. "You okay, Vi?"

I raise my hands in the air. "I'm fine, everyone. My boob took the brunt of the hit. Don't worry, Alex will kiss it better later." I scrunch up my face. "Dammit. I was doing so good with the non-embarrassing remarks today."

Alex's mouth twitches and he wraps one arm around my waist. "Let's get you dried off and I can check you for damage."

"I'm real sorry!" Pretty Eyes calls out as Alex guides me toward the pool house.

"Don't worry about it!" I call over my shoulder. "Wow. His eyes are really something else."

"You've mentioned that a few times now." Alex shuffles me into the pool house bedroom and closes the door. "Where did you get hit exactly?"

I point to my left boob and take a seat on the edge of the bed, soaking the comforter with my wet butt. "He doesn't wear contacts."

Alex arches an annoyed brow as he pulls the tie behind my neck, setting my boobs free.

"It's just an observation, and my boob is fine."

"I'm checking anyway."

"You just want to cop a feel."

"I want to make sure my teammate didn't damage my wife," he snaps and cups my boobs in his hands, thumbs brushing over my nipples.

"Alex," I breathe.

His eyes flip up to mine. "Does that hurt, baby?"

"No."

He bites his lip and does it again. "Does it feel good?"

I nod and arch a little. "Maybe you should kiss it better now instead of later."

"Maybe I should." He drops to his knees on the floor, edging his way between my legs, and brushes his lips against the swell, teasing me.

I run my fingers through his hair. "Alex?"

He lifts his gaze, lips barely grazing my skin. "Yeah, baby?"

"Your eyes are the prettiest."

He smiles and his tongue flicks out to touch my nipple.

Alex proceeds to do a full body exam, with his mouth. Turns out, I'm totally fine and 100% boneless by the time he's done.

MILF IN TRAINING
Violet

WHY DID I WRITE THIS? I wrote this for Dirty Blond Books this year for Valentine's Day. I've had A LOT of people wanting Violet & Alex becoming parents, because let's face it, it would be insane. So I sort of got us part of the way there with this ridiculous little outtake.

AFTER I PEE ON the stick and discover that Alex's super sperm have succeeded in impregnating me with what I'm expecting will be his superior athletic offspring, I spend the afternoon doing pretty much anything except work. I'd feel baddish, but I'm on salary and what I don't finish here I'll take care of at home.

Instead of managing my accounts, I look up creative ways to tell Alex he's going to be a dad. I find the perfect set of couple's shirts and order them express so I have them for when he arrives home tomorrow afternoon. I follow that up by ordering several throw pillows, a cake with a special inscription, and a personalized bottle of sparkling white grape juice.

At the end of the workday, in which I've completed little to no actual work, I head home with the intention of decorating the house for his arrival. I should have loads of time to accomplish this since his flight doesn't land until early afternoon tomorrow.

Except I'm super tired after a long day of being excited and a little terrified that a human life is growing inside my body. So instead of decorating, Charlene and I order takeout and look at cute baby stuff online until I pass out on her shoulder. She's kind enough to wake me up and forces me to go upstairs to my bed so I don't wake up with a crick in my neck. Charlene is a great bestie. If I have a girl, I hope she has a bestie who's as awesome as Char.

I sleep until noon the next day. I would've slept longer, but the doorbell keeps ringing. I grab the sleeve of soda crackers from the nightstand—apparently, it helps with morning sickness, which I don't have yet, but is supposed to hit around the eight-week mark—and get my ass out of bed so I can answer the door.

It isn't until I open the door that I remember I have a whole bunch of stuff arriving today, and it appears as though I've slept through several deliveries based on the number of boxes at my front door. The current delivery is the cake.

The delivery guy has a hard time making eye contact, which is my fault since I'm wearing a T-shirt with no bra that says HANDS GO HERE over my chest. I sign for the cake, send the delivery guy on his way, and carry the box carefully into the kitchen. I cry when I open it, because it's absolutely perfect. Also, I'm pregnant and everything makes me cry.

Aside from the text that reads *Super Sperm Gets the Job Done*, it's also decorated with a sperm wearing a cape. He's swimming toward an egg with her arms outstretched and heart eyes. I'm aware eggs don't have arms or eyes, but for the sake of the cake they do.

Once I get myself together, I bring in all the other items from the front porch. Then I sit down and drink half a gallon of orange juice because I'm thirsty and eat most of a sleeve of soda crackers because they taste okay and I'm too lazy to make anything else. While I eat, I open the rest of the boxes. The fake champagne label is inscribed with *Congratulations Alex! You knocked me up!*

Once I'm done with breakfast, I bring the throw pillows upstairs and arrange them on our bed, which really means I toss them in with the other seventy-five million pillows I've purchased since we got married. The new ones say *We Made a Baby Here* and *MOMMA to be* and *DADDY to be*.

It's already one in the afternoon and Alex will be home soon, so I get in the shower, clean all the sleep off my body, and prepare it for Alex's arrival. If I'd had time, I would've gotten my beaver bedazzled, but my new underpants will have to do. I did manage to get my nails done, though. They're yellow with little tiny diapers and bottles drawn on them.

By the time I'm done in the shower, I'm already wishing I could lie down and take a nap. I guess the whole pregnancy thing explains why I'm so tired all the time and why I've been falling asleep at eight o'clock every night.

I pull on a pair of leggings that Alex thinks are particularly flattering on my butt. Then I carefully wrangle my sensitive boobs into my new bra. I'm up another cup size, which sucks because now I'm at the point where I'll have to get them all custom made, and I've been told they'll only get bigger as pregnancy goes on.

I pull the shirt over my head and frown at how tight it is across my chest. Also, there's an insane amount of cleavage since it's a V-neck. Hmm. I guess I should've gone up a size. Oh well, it'll serve its purpose, and I assume it won't stay on long since Alex will likely want to celebrate his knocking me up with sexy times.

The sound of the alarm beeping downstairs signals that Alex is home. I cup my boobs and look at my reflection in the mirror. "Look alive, girls, we're about to drop the baby bomb!" I do a shimmy shake, then cringe, because that hurts.

I rush downstairs—carefully, though, because I'm not known for my coordination, and the last thing I need is to fall. I grab my purse from the bottom of the stairs and root around until I find the pregnancy test, which I quickly stick a bow on and set on top of the cake box in the kitchen.

I take a deep breath and head down the hall with the goal of intercepting Alex. The door connected to the garage swings open and Alex steps into the front foyer. He drops his bag and scoops me up in his arms, lifting me off the floor and crushing me to his chest. "God, it's so good to be home."

He nuzzles into my neck, lips moving along my jaw to my mouth. I don't even get a chance to tell him I missed him before his tongue is in my mouth and he's wrapping my legs around his waist. I indulge in the mouth fucking, because Alex is a fantastic kisser. He kneads my ass as he carries me across the foyer. I realize he's headed for the stairs, which will totally mess up my plan, so I cup his cheeks and disengage our mouths long enough to say, rather breathlessly, "Kitchen."

Alex smirks. "Feel like a little counter fucking, eh, baby? Does that mean you bedazzled your beaver for me again? Wait. Don't tell me. I want it to be a surprise." Annnndddd . .

. we're back to the mouth fucking.

Alex is so focused on making out that he doesn't notice the elaborate setup as he drops me on the counter. He yanks his shirt over his head and tosses it on the floor. Then he cups my boobs, covering the majority of the lettering decorating them, and lowers his head. "Fuck, I missed you." His voice is muffled by my cleavage.

"Alex." It's part moan, part protest. My nipples are super sensitive these days.

"Is it just me or are your boobs bigger?" He backs up a little and gives them a gentle squeeze. "Is this a new bra? What does your shirt say?"

"You'll have to let go of my boobs so you can read it." I grab hold of his wrists and encourage him to release them. He's understandably reluctant.

He reads the words stamped across my chest, brow pulling together as his lips turn down. "*MILF in Training*?" He drags his eyes away from my chest and arches a brow.

Usually my husband is smart, but it's obvious his hormones are in control right now, and the head below the belt is doing all the thinking for him. I reach behind me, which happens to make my chest jut out, and feel around for the pregnancy test. I hold it up in front of his face and say, "Tada!"

"What do I need a pen for right now?"

I check to make sure that's not what I'm holding. "It's not a pen, Alex." I shove it between my boobs since that's where he's looking.

He plucks it aggressively from my cleavage, slightly annoyed, and pries the bow off. It takes about two and a half seconds before he reacts. His eyes go wide and his mouth drops open when it finally registers that he's holding a pregnancy test. With a blue plus sign. He brings it closer to his face, inspecting the little box where those lines intersect each other.

"Baby?" His gaze flips up to mine and then back down to the pregnancy test, then to my boobs and back to my face. "Vi? Does this mean what I think it means?"

"If you think it means that your super sperm have managed to swim the mighty beaver channel and you managed to knock me up, then the answer is yes." I really wish I had my phone on me, because his expression is priceless and getting a video of this moment would've been epic. Too bad I'm already suffering from baby brain and all my best ideas happen when it's too late to do anything about it.

"You're pregnant?"

"According to that test I am."

"This isn't a joke, right? This isn't like one of Sunny's old tests and you're just doing this to get me all excited?"

I make a face. "Uh, no, Alex, I'm not touching something your sister has peed on."

"How accurate are these?" He waves the pee stick around in the air.

"A hundred percent."

"So you're really pregnant?" He blinks four thousand times in a row, like he's halfway between crying and freaking out with excitement.

"I'm really pregnant." I watch his expression shift as the news finally, truly sets in.

Alex's grin lights up the entire world. Man, my husband is pretty. "We're having a baby!"

I return his smile. "How do you feel about that, Alex?"

"I feel fuckin' awesome! This is better than winning The

Cup!" He fist pumps and follows it with, "Fuck yeah!"

He places a palm over my still mostly flat belly, eyes alight with excitement usually reserved for my bare boobs. "I'm gonna be a dad!"

"You are, and you're going to be amazing."

And I know without a doubt that's true, because he puts a hundred and ten percent into everything he loves.

KICK STAND KID

WHY DID I WRITE THIS? You'll find out at the end, because I don't want to spoil this for you ;)

I CAN'T FIND MY WIFE.

Normally, this isn't much of a worry, but she's very, very pregnant. She's also five days overdue and pretty desperate to get this baby out. Her car is in the garage, though, and she didn't mention going anywhere today, so she has to be around here somewhere.

It's possible she's napping. It's also possible she's gotten herself stuck somewhere. Last week, she got trapped in the living room lounger and had to resort to texting me for help. I tried not to laugh, but I failed. Boobgate went into effect until I bought her apology flowers and her favorite non-dairy shake. Violet has been craving a lot of ice cream during this pregnancy, which is not ideal since she can't handle lactose.

I call her name for the tenth time as I head upstairs. I check the most obvious places first. Our bedroom is empty and our bed is made, the bathroom door is open and there's no Violet in there, and she's not in the nursery or her sewing room either. I check the guest bedrooms and bathrooms just in case, but still no Violet.

I head back downstairs, my concern growing. I check the office, but again, no wife. I continue down the hall, past my workout room to the library. Which is exactly where I find her. Doing something she definitely shouldn't be considering her current state. She has earbuds in, which accounts for the reason she couldn't hear me calling her name.

She must catch the movement in the doorway out of the corner of her eye because she glances my way and startles, dropping the armful of books she's carrying. "Shit!" she yells, then starts hopping around, smashing into the waist high towers of books arranged in haphazard piles around her.

The domino effect is rapid and impressive. One tower goes over, knocking into the next one and then the next.

"No! Oh God, no!" Violet tries to save the next pile from going over, but all she succeeds in doing is causing the ones behind her to tumble when she bumps them with her butt.

Within thirty seconds, all but one of the book towers has fallen. Her face crumples and she bursts into tears. "I organized it all for nothing!" She lowers herself to the floor, slowly. It's more of an actual crouch and a gentle plop, but it still causes the remaining tower to fall.

Here's the thing about my wife. She's not usually super dramatic. Quirky? Yes, which is one of the traits I love most about her. She also says what's on her mind when it's on her mind, something else I love about her, even if it means sometimes she says things that embarrass her.

But pregnant Violet is a whole different story. She's not only dramatic, she's also emotional and hormonal.

Individually, I can handle any of those things. The hormonal part I manage exceedingly well. I'm more than happy to service my wife and her needs as often as she likes. Which has been very, very often all throughout this pregnancy. I'm also aware as soon as this baby comes I will no longer have access to the boobs, or the rest of her for a while, so I will take what I can get when I can get it.

The emotional side of my wife is something I've had to learn how to deal with because she's generally not much of a crier. Sure, when we went through a rough patch back when we were dating and I was an asshole, there were tears. And when I had that accident and ended up in the hospital with a severe concussion, there were more tears, but other than that, she's really pretty level.

At least until I got her pregnant. Now she cries at tissue commercials, or cute stuffed animals—pretty much anything will bring the waterworks, really. And with her being five days overdue, she's extra sensitive.

"Baby, what're you doing?" I carefully step over the mountain of books surrounding her.

"I was organizing books until you came in here and ruined it all!" she sobs.

"But the books were already organized." We used the Dewey Decimal System to set them up. Every shelf is organized based on book genre and then they're alphabetized. Violet insisted on it.

"All the romance books weren't organized by sub-genre, though. The contemporary romance was in with paranormal romance and the new adult fiction and the classics. It was all wrong. I needed to fix it. And Sunny said exercise will help get this baby out. I just want to be able to see my vagina again. That's all. And my feet without sitting down." She dashes away the tears. "Look at this mess! And I'm too tired to clean it up now." Her shoulders slump and she exhales a long, exasperated breath as she rubs her belly.

"Come on, baby. I know it's comfy in there, but I really want you to come out so we can meet you. And so I can see my feet again and Alex can stop worrying that he's poking you in the spine every time we have sex." Her head snaps up. "We should have sex. Maybe an orgasm will get him out." She grabs the hem of my shirt and starts pulling it over my head.

"Do you want to go upstairs? The bed will be more comfortable." My words are muffled by fabric.

"Let's be spontaneous and have sex here."

"Okay." I'm not going to argue with Violet, not when she's offering sex and she's so emotionally reactive.

Now that Violet has decided she wants to have sex, she's on a mission to get me naked. My shirt is still half on and covering my face, but she abandons it and goes for my belt. I pull my shirt off and toss it aside. She pops the button on my jeans, unzips them halfway, and then pushes my pants and boxers down. I'm already mostly hard, so my erection gets caught in the fabric.

Violet reaches in and frees me from my boxers. I groan at the sight of her perfectly manicured nails, one of which has my jersey number painted on it, wrapped around my shaft.

She leans in and presses a kiss to the tip. "I really need you to work superpowers on my vagina and give me an orgasm, Super MC."

"I'll give you more than one," I promise as I help her out of her shirt and unclasp her bra, setting her boobs free. I cup them and very carefully nuzzle between them. "I love you."

"Are you talking to my boobs or me?" I can hear Violet's

brow arching.

"Both." I kiss each nipple, then suck them, but gently because Violet's boobs are ultra sensitive these days. She gasps, then grabs my hair and moans when I do it again.

I finish undressing her and try to find a place to lay her down, but fallen books surround us.

"Wait." She puts a hand on my chest. "I can't lie on these! I might bend the covers!" Violet is a little weird about the state of her books. She hates it when her paperbacks have creases in the spines or dog-eared covers.

"We can move to the couch? Or I can take you upstairs?" I figure giving her the option of a bed again is smart.

"I guess the couch is still spontaneous."

"Totally spontaneous and far more comfortable than the floor." I help her up and we navigate our way out of the circle of books. Once she's sitting down, I drop to my knees between her thighs and kiss her.

"I can't wait until I can see my vagina without a mirror again." She moans when I circle her clit with a finger, dragging it down and easing inside her. It doesn't take me long to make her come. I pull her to the edge of the couch and give her a second orgasm with my mouth. Then I position myself between her thighs and rub a few extra circles on her sensitive clit. "Is this position good for you, baby? Are you comfortable?"

"I have a bowling ball in my stomach. I'm never comfortable, Alex, but this works. I can sort of see what's going on down there."

I ease in, slowly, groaning at how insanely tight she is. I don't mention that, though, because Violet is terrified that she's going to end up with a baggy vagina—her words— after this baby comes out. So I go with, "You feel so good."

It's true, and a lot safer.

I'm about halfway in when Violet says, "You know what? I changed my mind."

I hold my position. "What?"

"This feels too much like a birthing position. It's messing with my head. Maybe I should be on top."

I'm relieved that she hasn't changed her mind about sex entirely because finishing myself off by hand isn't as appealing as finishing inside my wife. Also, I'm highly aware that once this baby comes I won't be allowed inside her for a while. Weeks probably. And I don't think she's going to be interested in giving me consolation blow jobs either. "Sure. Okay. Do you want me to sit on the couch, or I can lie down?"

"Sitting up is probably best, right? Then you can love on my boobs, too."

We switch positions. It takes a bit for Violet to get comfortable. At first, her knees keep sliding between the cushions. Eventually, we get everything lined up and I get back inside her.

I nuzzle her boobs and hold onto her ass while she rides me. "I can't wait until we can have headboard banging sex again," she moans. I know she's about to come again when she starts chanting her cock love.

When it's my turn, I hold her hips and move her over me, faster, but not harder, until I come, too.

Violet eventually lifts her head from my shoulder. "I don't think it worked."

"You don't think what worked?"

"The sex. I don't think it triggered labor." She sighs. "Maybe we need to have it again."

"Sure, baby. I'm more than happy to keep trying until it works." What can I say, I'm a selfless giver.

Violet

I wake up for the five billionth time because I have to pee. It's three in the morning and Alex is passed out beside me. Sleeping peacefully. Not having to pee. I throw the covers off and roll out of bed. I'm halfway to the bathroom when a rush of warmth hits my underwear and then starts dripping down my thighs.

At first, I think I've peed myself, until I remember that I'm super overdue and that I've been waiting for this moment, because it means my water has broken. I watch as an impressive puddle forms at my feet. It's good that we have hardwood floors. Otherwise, this would be gross to clean up. I imagine fluid that's been hanging out in my uterus for forty weeks isn't particularly appealing.

"Alex!"

He bolts upright in bed. "I can be hard in thirty seconds. Just let me hold your boobs."

"I don't want sex. The baby's coming."

He leans over and fumbles around with the lamp on the nightstand, nearly knocking everything else off in the process. He blinds himself when he finally manages to turn it on and blinks a bunch of times before finally focusing on me. "What? Really? Like now?"

"Like now," I confirm.

Shit. This is really happening. I'm having this baby. I'm going to push something significantly larger than my husband's huge peen out of my vagina. What the hell was I thinking when I said we could have a baby?

The first real contraction happens then. It's like I'm Kegeling and having period cramps at the same time. "Oh!" I put both hands on my belly.

Alex goes from half-asleep to complete panic in about four seconds flat. "Are you okay? What's wrong? I need to get the bag. We have to get to the hospital now!"

He rushes over to me, excited and freaking out, but his expression shifts to confusion as he grabs my shoulders and looks down. "Why is the floor wet?"

"My water broke. You're standing in baby juice."

We both make a face, because that sounds horrible. Thankfully, he ignores it and pulls me into a hug. "We're going to meet our baby! The one we made. Together."

"Because we like to get our fuck on a lot," I add.

He kisses me, without tongue, and then hugs me again. "We should go, shouldn't we?"

"Uh, I think we're supposed to wait until the contractions are like four minutes apart, or something, aren't we? And we both need to get dressed. I'm thinking maybe I'd like to have a shower and wash all the baby water off me. And we should clean up the floor so no one slips."

"Right. Okay. You stay here and I'll get a towel." Alex rushes to the bathroom and returns five seconds later with a towel.

Once the slipping hazard is cleaned up, he helps me to the bathroom and turns on the shower. I have two contractions while I'm taking my last shower as a pregnant woman. They're not that bad. I can totally deal with labor if this is what it's like.

By the time I get out, Alex is already dressed, my bag is

ready, and my delivery outfit is laid out on the bed for me.

Alex is too antsy to wait for my contractions to be four minutes apart, so once I'm dressed, we head to the hospital. Turns out, the timing is actually pretty good, because things speed up once I'm in the car, and by the time we get to the hospital, the contractions are significantly closer together and a hell of a lot more painful.

Alex is like a very concerned, but annoying mother bird, fluttering around me, asking if he can do anything to help.

"Maybe never jizz inside me again," I groan as another contraction forces me to grip the railing and try to breathe through the pain.

"I'm sorry it hurts. Maybe you should practice your breathing. That's supposed to help, isn't it?" Alex starts doing the Lamaze breathing exercises. Normally, I'd think this is sweet, but right now I'm in too much pain to be nice.

When I can't take more than five steps without having a contraction, Alex takes me back to the room, apologizing a thousand times until I snap at him for that, too, which makes me feel bad, so I start crying.

Turns out, tears and labor get a lot of attention, as does Alex, being who he is, so a flock of nurses swarm the room.

"I'd like the epidural now, please," I tell the one who looks like Betty from *The Golden Girls*.

"We'll just check to see how dilated you are first." She pats my hand and then moves into position at the end of the bed so she and all her nurse teammates can check out the state of my cooch. "Oh, you're ready to go! Let's get the doctor in here." She looks up from my vagina and smiles. "You're going to have your baby now."

"But what about the epidural?" My voice is so shrill it probably sounds like a dog whistle.

"Oh, honey, you're too far along for that. Don't you worry, you'll be just fine."

"Fine? No, no, no. I'm not going to be fine. I hate pain and this—" the next contraction steals my ability to speak for as long as it lasts, "—really fucking hurts!"

I look over at Alex, whose hand I'm gripping, but his eyes are not on my face. They're homed in between my legs, wide with shock. I squeeze even harder on his hand and he flinches, gaze flipping up to mine. "You got this, baby," he croaks.

Another horrible contraction hits me and I groan and try to breathe through it. "My mom is such a liar," I say through gritted teeth. "Labor pains are not like period cramps. It feels like The Hulk is trying to burst out of my body."

Alex smooths my hair off my face. I'm sure he's ready to issue another apology, but the doctor arrives, all smiles, looking happy as a pig in shit. He claps his hands enthusiastically. "Looks like it's time to have a baby!"

I would like to say I'm quiet about my pain, and that I'm a badass when it comes to giving birth, but I'm not. I yell and grunt and tell Alex he's never allowed near me with Super MC again. "I hope you enjoy the feel of your hand for the rest of your goddamn life," I growl at him between pushes.

And like the sweet, patient Canadian he is, he tells me how sorry he is. He also puts on his team captain hat and tells me I'm doing a great job and that he's so proud of me. I appreciate it as much as I'm able, considering how freaking much giving birth hurts.

Finally, I'm given the "one big push" order by the doctor, who also asks Alex if he'd like to see the baby's head come out.

I squeeze his hand. "Do not look at my beaver right now, Alex. I don't want you to end up with vag destruction PTSD. I just want you to remember how pretty it was before I pushed something abnormally large out of it."

Thankfully, he listens to me and not the doctor. I push one last time and finally the head appears, and then everything is a hell of a lot easier, but still really damn painful as baby Robbie finally bursts out.

I flop back on the bed, really damn tired because pushing a baby out is hard work. Alex kisses me on the forehead. "You did so good, Vi. I'm so proud of you."

The nurses are gathered around the doctor. My legs are still open, demoed lady bits on display. A tiny cry fills the room as baby Robbie (they better not have made a mistake about it being a boy) takes his first breath.

"Wow, that's just . . ." one of the nurses mutters.

"Good God!" the other one says, then lowers her voice to whisper something to the doctor.

"It's like a kick stand," the second nurse chimes in.

What the hell are they talking about?

"Is everything okay? Is our baby okay?" I struggle to sit up, wanting to see whatever it is they're seeing.

One of the nurses glances over at us and smiles. Her cheeks are bright pink. "Oh yes! Everything is just fine. You have a perfectly healthy baby boy. Some woman is going to be very lucky one day."

Alex and I exchange a look, because neither of us knows what the hell the nurse is talking about. And honestly, he's just been born. I don't want to start thinking about the day he starts dating and we have to have the sex talk. My mom gave me a vibrator and told me I should learn how to give myself an orgasm before I let anyone else try it. Not bad advice, really, but still so awkward.

The nurse who's busy cleaning off our baby holds him up so we can see what's causing all the commotion at the end of the birthing bed.

"Oh, thank God." I squeeze Alex's hand, and he grimaces, probably because I've been using it like a stress ball for my entire delivery. "He's got your peen." I address the nurse who's now swaddling our baby in a blue blanket. "I was so worried he wasn't going to take after his dad since my biological father apparently had a smaller than average peen. So this is great news. Here's hoping the Waters' genetics win out in all the other important areas."

Interestingly enough, no one comments on that.

I notice a bunch of things I probably shouldn't as she passes me our son. I cradle him in my arms and stroke the short dark hair on his tiny cone-shaped head. "Is his head going to stay like this? He looks kind of like a gnome, or maybe an alien. Look at how puffy his eyes are. It's like he's been smoking the green demon while he was waiting to be born."

The nurse assures me that his head will round out, which is a relief, and that his eyes won't be so puffy in a couple of days and he'll look more human and a lot less like he's been smoking reefer.

"He's perfect," Alex says. "We made something beautiful, didn't we?"

I think he has daddy blinders on, but I have to agree, that despite the cone head and the reefer eyes, he's pretty damn adorable.

"Do you have a name picked out?" one of the nurses asks.

Alex leans over and kisses his tiny little forehead, and then he kisses my sweaty one. "Robert Sidney Waters, but we'll call him Robbie."

***A LOT of readers have asked for Violet giving birth, because it's Violet and everything she does is insane, so I felt this year everyone deserved to see what it would be like for her to shoot a baby out of her beaver. It's not pretty and she's not graceful about it. This is Violet and Alex. And honestly, labor is not a walk in a meadow on a sunny day. It's a lot of work and your vagina is angry for a while afterwards.

WHY DID I WRITE THIS? Every year I write love letters on Valentine's Day, so the year after I released Pucked Off, I felt like everyone needed to see that these two were doing okay, because let's face it, Lance was a mess and he's lucky as hell that he found Poppy.

Pretty Poppy.

I should've felt bad when I stole your first kiss all those years ago, but I didn't then, not the way I should have, and I definitely don't feel bad about it now. Not when you're my brightest star and my warmest sun. You're everything good and right in this world and I'm constantly amazed that you're mine.

You did some stealing of your own that night, without either of us knowing it. You took my heart with you and I didn't know it was missing until I found you again. You can keep it forever, though. I don't mind since you take such good care of it. You put my soul back together with your sweetness and your kindness and your strength.

You'll always be my first and only love.
XO Lance

POPPY & LANCE
(THE DELETED SCENES)

I DEBATED WHETHER OR not to include this. It's more than 5000 words of deleted scenes from Pucked Off. I've said this many times in conversation and I believe in written response, but when I wrote Pucked Off, it was very much a compulsion. Sometimes I would have scenes in my head that I just needed to get down, and they wouldn't always come in order.

This outtake is one of those scenes in which I had an idea for what would be a confrontation with Tash and Lance's implosion, but when I was tying the story together, it didn't fit and Tash was her own drama. We didn't necessarily need more of her, so this scene hit the cutting room floor.

I think had I included this scene you may have seen a very different side of Lance, one that would have been a lot harder to manage, because he is a very damaged man, and a lot of Poppy's fears are real and honest. Lance is a victim who doesn't know how to escape the cycle of abuse, and while I feel like the way I told his story and Poppy's stayed true to my vision, writing this scene helped me see him for exactly who he was, and exactly how strong a heroine Poppy had to be to love him as much as she did, with such conviction.

Everyone deserves to be loved without conditions or pain.

THE PARTY
Poppy

I'M STILL SITTING IN my car down the block from Lance's place when headlights start to flicker on around me. A swarm of people come from the direction of Lance's house, taking up the entire sidewalk. I roll down my window a crack and catch some of the conversation as they pass.

"I don't know what happened . . ."

"I've heard he loses it like that sometimes."

"Sucks that he kicked everyone out—"

"—Hope we get invited back again."

Car doors open, numbers are exchanged, and people make plans to head to local bars. Engines rev to life and cars pass me as I sit there, until the street is virtually empty. I guess the party is over, and I have to wonder what exactly was the impetus for that. I'm not egotistical enough to think it's me, but I'm suddenly starting to regret the way I reacted to this entire situation.

I have no idea what his history is with that woman, but I assume whatever it is, it can't be good, or simple, because nothing about Lance is. Well, there are good parts, but nothing is really simple based on my experience so far.

I sit in my car for another minute or two before I decide that maybe I should reconsider whether or not I want to leave. Despite everything that's happened, I know that none of it was intentional up to this point. Not the night at the bar, not what happened with Kristi. I wasn't honest with him from the beginning, so it's not fair for me to put this all on him.

What I'm having the most difficulty with is the knowledge that so many of the rumors I've heard over the years appear to be true. I don't know what to do with that, because I've seen that side of him that made me fall in love with the idea of a boy so many years ago. I know he's in there. I just don't know what happened to turn him into this man with two sides, one I'm not sure I want to manage.

I stay there for a few more seconds, debating my options. I could go home and never talk to him again. It wouldn't be hard. Or I could go back there and see if there's something worth staying for. Eventually, I turn off the engine and get out of the car. It's cold out, so I pull the edges of my sweater closed and rush along the sidewalk, back to his house.

It isn't Lance who answers the door. It's Randy. I hate the look of pity on his face.

"Can I talk to him?"

Randy sighs. "He's not in good form right now, Poppy."

"I was just here fifteen minutes ago, and he seemed fine then." This isn't quite true. He didn't seem fine at all, but I still want to see him, because I feel like I'm part of the reason for him not being okay.

"It's really not a good idea."

"Why not?"

"Who the fuck is here? Is it Tash? Tell her to fuck off. I'm done with her shit." There's a distinct slur in Lance's voice.

"You should really go, Poppy. He wouldn't want you to see him like this."

"Like what?" I push past Randy and he steps away from the door, allowing me into the house.

The table that usually holds a vase of flowers—something I found strange, considering a hockey player lives here alone—is surrounded with broken fragments of glass.

"What happened?" I ask, moving farther into the house as I go in search of Lance. He can't be too far away.

The sound of glass breaking startles me and Randy runs a hand over his face. He grabs my arm as I turn in the direction of the noise. "You really don't want to see this, Poppy."

I wrench my arm out of his grip and head for the living room. What I find is a lot more than a broken glass. The coffee table has been overturned, the glass top shattered all over the floor. And that's just the beginning of the damage. It looks like the place has been ransacked from a break-in. But it's clear that isn't what happened, because in the middle of the ruin is the man I'm here to see.

"Lance?"

He spins around. I can see he's struggling to focus on me, he's so drunk.

"Poppy? What're you doin' 'ere?"

"I wanted to talk to you," I say meekly.

He shakes his head vigorously and waves the bottle in his hand around, sloshing amber liquid onto the floor. "You shouldn't be here." He trains his unsteady, angry gaze on Randy and he stumbles through the debris toward me. "You shouldna let 'er in."

As I survey the wreckage, I have to wonder if I can handle any of this. This is a broken man I'm dealing with. He's not a fifteen-year-old boy kissing me in a closet for the first time. He's a grown man whose past haunts him in a way I still don't understand and it makes him volatile. It's right for me to worry that one day I'm going to end up on the receiving end of his hostility. And then where will I be? Who will I be but a victim that allowed herself to become one?

I should leave. I should walk away.

But I don't.

Because it's what he expects me to do, and if I abandon him now, I'm leaving everyone else to clean up the mess. One I've helped create.

I step carefully around broken glass, and when I'm close enough, I take the bottle from his hand and set it on the closest table. "Let me see your hands," I say softly.

He holds them out for me. His knuckles are shredded and bloody.

"You shouldn't have come back. You were right to go. I'm not a good person, Poppy. My head—" He taps his temple. "—It's all messed up."

I ignore the part about him being messed up. I don't know if he's referencing his current state or if he means in a more permanent way. The things I know about this man lead me to believe it's the latter, and it makes me sad that he feels this way about himself. "We should get you cleaned up, don't you think?"

I gently take his hand and lead him toward the staircase. I've never been to his room, although I know exactly where it is in this house, having stood outside the door wishing I could get my things and go that night over a year ago.

Lance doesn't protest. He just lets me guide him to his room. He's unsteady on his feet, bumping into the wall and me as we go. His room is mostly tidy, although a small pile of clothes lies in a rumpled heap on the floor near his closet. A towel hangs over the edge of his huge king-sized bed, and the sheets are messed up on one side, like maybe he'd taken a nap.

I keep going, walking all the way to the other side, to the bathroom. "Do you have a first aid kit in your bathroom?"

His nod is sloppy.

I push the door open and flick on the light. Shaving instruments are scattered on the white marble top. Towels lie discarded on the floor after a shower. His toothpaste has the cap left off, another sign he was distracted or in a rush, or maybe it's not something he cares all that much about.

I flip the toilet seat lid down and give it a pat. "Have a seat."

"I should clean up." He waves a loose hand over the counter.

"You can worry about that later."

"You need me to do anything for you?" Randy asks from the doorway. His hands are shoved into his pockets and he looks uncomfortable standing where he is.

"Maybe just the mess downstairs. I've got Lance from here, right now."

He hesitates for a few seconds, his gaze flicking between Lance and me, maybe assessing whether he's going to lose it again. I've yet to bear witness to his outbursts, but I've seen enough of his fights on the ice to know what his rage looks like.

"I can manage this," I assure him.

He leaves Lance and me alone. I turn on the water and move the shaving stuff aside. "We should wash your hands."

Lance steps up behind me, pressing his chest against my back. He wraps his arms around me and drops his face into my hair. I freeze for a few prolonged seconds, staring at our reflections in the mirror. He's massive compared to me with a good foot and a hundred pounds of sculpted muscle filling out his frame. For the first time, I wonder if I should be afraid of him, and the thought makes me sad.

I lift my hands, covering his thick forearms as he tightens his hold on me, burying is face deeper into my hair. He's muttering something, but I can't make out what he's saying.

"Lance?"

He makes a sound into my neck. And then I feel the press of his lips. All the right, corresponding parts respond accordingly. My nipples tighten, my stomach clenches, and warmth floods low and heavy between my legs.

Nothing is going to happen between us tonight. He's drunk and uncoordinated, not to mention emotionally on the edge. But I let him hold me for a little while longer before I coax him to loosen his grip and move his bloody hands under the warm spray. I pump out some soap and run my palm gently over his knuckles.

Lance keeps his face buried in my hair. His lips are still against my neck and now I can feel his hard-on against my lower back. I ignore it and keep working, switching hands to get rid of the dry, crusted blood so I can properly assess the damage.

When I'm done, I pat them dry with the hand towel. He starts to wrap them around me again, but I put my arms up to bar the action.

Lance lifts his head, finally, and gives me a bleary, questioning look. There's anger under the surface, but sadness and rejection dominate.

"Let me take care of your hands."

He drops them and steps back enough that I can turn

around, but not without brushing against him. When I do, his hard-on rubs against my stomach through his pants. He looks anything but apologetic as he stares down at me. There's a wall up right now, guarding emotions he fights to contain. I see that now. I see a lot of things I didn't want to until now.

His fingers brush mine and then his palms travel up my arms, a barely there whisper of touch. Up, up, up he goes, sweeping my hair back over my shoulders. His fingertips skim the sides of my neck, and then he frames my face with his hands—not touching, just hovering. They're shaking. I can feel the vibration against my skin every time they make accidental contact.

"You're so perfect," he mutters. "I'm not good enough."

"Of course, you are," I whisper.

He gives his head a slow shake. "I'm really not." With a heavy sigh he moves over to the toilet and drops down on the seat. Resting his elbow on his knee, he props the other arm up on the counter, giving me access to his raw knuckles.

"Where's your first aid kit?" I ask.

He points to a set of cupboard doors. I open it and find neatly stacked towels, a shelf of hair supplies, and other random bathroom items.

"It's on the top shelf. You need me to get it for you?"

"I've got it." I stretch up on my tiptoes and snag the handle, pulling down the kit. I set it beside him on the counter and flip it open. I find the antiseptic wipes and tear one open. Taking his hand in mine, I dab at his knuckles.

"You don't need to be gentle. I can handle the pain."

I glance up to find him watching me. "I'm sure you can, but it doesn't mean you have to endure it."

He huffs a little and smiles. "I'm good at it."

"A little too good if you ask me." I wipe across his

knuckles again and blow across them.

"What're you doing?"

"Taking out the sting." When all I get is a confused look, I continue with an explanation. "Didn't your mom ever do that when you were a kid and you hurt yourself?"

"I dealt with that stuff on my own, or my nanny did."

"Even when you were really little?"

"From what I remember, yeah." He shrugs. "My mom wasn't big on that part."

He'd mentioned before how he and his mom weren't close, and that he pretty much only saw her once a year, during the holidays.

I refocus on the cuts on his knuckles. Scars litter the back of his hands, ones that look old, and others that haven't turned white quite yet. He's been in a lot of fights on the ice, and based on the state of his living room, that aggression isn't isolated.

"How often does this happen?"

"The parties? I haven't had as many lately since all my close friends have girlfriends and wives and the bunnies can be a real problem."

My stomach clenches. I have no idea what he wants out of this, which probably makes me stupid.

"I mean this." I tap the back of his hand. "But I can see how that would create some conflict."

"Tash wasn't invited tonight. She just showed up."

"It's really not my business."

"Sure it is. I invited you, not her. She's always trying to screw with me."

"Why?"

"Because it's what she does."

"This is the woman who used to be your team trainer?

The one who got fired?" Lance's arm twitches and his knee bobs. He's drunk and edgy. "You don't have to talk about it." This probably isn't a good time to have this conversation, anyway.

"I tried to make it something it wasn't with her and things got complicated. Now she won't stop making things difficult."

"Difficult how?"

"She always calls when she's in town, even though I've told her not to. Shows up when she's not invited, tries to get under my skin and succeeds, obviously." He wiggles his fingers.

"That's quite an impact she has." I move to the other hand, sinking to the floor so it's easier for both of us. I kneel before him on the plush mat covering the hard tile and rest a palm on his thigh to steady myself. "Sorry." I rush to move it away, unsure what level of contact is going to be acceptable for him right now, in this state.

Lance covers my hand with his. "It's you, so it's okay." He drags his damp fingers along the backs of mine and he slips his thumb under my palm. Then he lifts my hand and brings it to his cheek, holding his palm against mine to keep it there. I still don't understand what makes me different from everyone else, but I know it's not good that I like this dependency he seems to have on me. Or that I want it to continue.

He drags my fingers over his lips. "Why'd you come back?"

"Because I didn't feel good about how things happened. I don't think people give you much of a chance, or maybe you expect that people won't, but I didn't want to be that person for you, or another person like that in your life."

"So you came back because you feel sorry for me?"

"I came back because I care."

"About me?" And there he is, that boy I met so many years ago, the one who set a timer in the closet, the one who was honest with me about not being sorry for stealing my first kiss. This man who mows down people on the ice and throws epic temper tantrums that result in the destruction of his own property looks so uncertain right now. And hopeful. And scared.

"Yes. Lance. About you."

"Why?"

"Because I see who you are."

"I'm not a good person."

"Yes, you are."

"I didn't recognize you."

"We were kids."

"I should've known who you were." He raises the other hand and taps his temple. "I don't remember much about that night, but I remember seeing you and thinking about how I wanted you."

"That's all you remember?"

"I get flashes. Sometimes when I'm with you the memories come back. And right now, 'cause I'm drunk. It's like that theory about remembering things when you're in the same state." He drops my hand and there's pain in his expression, an agony I'm familiar with. "What did I do the night you were here?" He runs a palm down his face. Blinking hard a few times, he shakes his head, like he's trying to understand the memory. "Did I invite you?"

"You didn't know—"

"Fuck. *Fuck.*" He presses his palm against his forehead and gives it a couple of taps before he lifts his gaze to me again. "Why are you here? Why would you want anything to do with me?"

I cringe as the reality of this thing between us finally comes crashing down.

"I just don't understand. Why would you let me near you when I'd done something so fucking horrible to you?"

"Because you weren't the person who did that when we were together."

"I'm always that person, Poppy."

"That's not true."

"Yes, it is." He holds up his hands. "This. This is what I do. I ruin shit. Myself, my stuff." He gestures to me. "You."

"You haven't ruined me."

"Come the fuck on, Poppy. Look at what I'm dragging you into. I don't have control over this. Myself. Anything. And here you are, willing to do what? Take care of me? Make me better? You're gonna get tired of this shit. I do."

He was voicing all my fears, everything I didn't want to face. I sit back on my heels, clasping my hands in my lap. What I should want and what I do want don't match. "Do you want me to go?"

"I should."

My heart skips in my chest. "But you don't?"

"No. You see now why I'm an asshole?"

"Would it be better if you kept wanting Tash instead?"

"For you, yeah."

"But not for you?"

"She's what I deserve. You're what I want to deserve."

"You keep saying things like that, but I don't understand where exactly you get the logic from. Everyone makes bad choices, Lance. You can't define yourself only by the worst decisions you make."

"I've done a lot of bad things."

"In whose eyes?"

"Mine. Yours if you knew about them."

"What's the worst thing you've done?"

"You don't want to know the answer to that."

I'm sure he's right, but I know a lot about his past already. It's splashed all over the media and in all the bunny groups.

"It's not just about making bad decisions, Poppy. It's that I keep making the same ones over and over again."

"Like what?"

"Like with Tash, I knew I was never going to get what I wanted from her, but I kept pushing for it anyway. And she kept messing with me, making me think maybe there was a chance, and then she'd take it away, but I'd go back the next time anyway, because I don't learn."

"But you haven't seen her in a while, right? Not before tonight?" I don't know how I'll manage if I don't get the answer I want.

"Not since I had to come to you for a massage. That was the last time."

"She did that to you?"

"No, seeing her made me stupid and I got into a bar fight."

"What happened?"

"She brought me something to share."

"What kind of something?"

"A girl."

I can only imagine the expression on my face. "Why would she do that?"

"Because that's what she likes and that's what she thought I'd like."

"And you didn't?"

Lance sighs. "People have a lot of preconceived ideas about me, and most of them are understandable. I know what kind of reputation I have and I've done more than enough to earn it, but just because I do the things I do, doesn't mean I always like that it's the way it has to be."

"Did she know that?"

"That I didn't want anyone but her? Yeah, but she didn't want the same thing, so it didn't ever go quite the way I wanted it to."

"How did you deal with that?"

Lance lifts one shoulder. "The way she expected me to."

I want to ask what that means, but I don't push for more answers, because I know what he'll tell me and I don't know if I'm ready to hear it, even if I already know the truth.

"I'm sorry."

"Why? You didn't do anything wrong."

"Because she hurt you, and it sounds like it was intentional." I pick up a new antiseptic wipe and tear it open, then go to work on the other hand.

Lance doesn't so much as flinch while I'm cleaning the wounds. When I'm done, I put antibacterial cream on them and wrap them with gauze.

"I'm going to get you some aspirin and some water, then I think it's lights out for you." I use the edge of the vanity to pull myself up.

"I can get it." He tries to pull himself up as well, but sways and ends up dropping back down on the closed toilet seat.

"Why don't you let me get this?"

"There's aspirin in the medicine cabinet and I've got a glass right there." He points to the counter.

I fill the glass and root through his medicine cabinet. I

drop two pills in his hand.

"I'll need a bit more than that."

"One more?"

"Two would be better."

I drop one more in his palm. "If you're still feeling bad in an hour, I'll give you more."

He tosses the pills into his mouth and swallows them down with a couple of gulps of water. "You're not leaving?"

"Do you want me to?"

"No."

"Then I'll stay."

"Why?"

"Stop asking questions you won't remember the answers to in the morning." I run my fingers through his hair, pushing it back off his forehead. "Now finish that so I can fill it again for you."

"I really hope I don't forget all of this." He does what I ask and drains the rest of the glass.

I WAS NEVER IN love with Tash. I know that with absolute certainty now. I cared about her. But we weren't good for each other, not the way I wanted us to be.

Poppy is a different story. It's been four days. They've been the longest four days of my fucking life. I feel like a junkie in withdrawal. I'm edgy and raw. I can't keep my shit together on the ice.

I almost managed to get a game suspension last night. In three days, I'm leaving for another short series of away games. I'll be gone for four days. I asked Coach if I could have a different roommate; I can't deal with Rookie and the bunnies. Also, punching him in the face and the whole shitshow with Tash wasn't much help. A little separation is a good thing.

I'm currently sitting in Waters' kitchen, having been invited for dinner, along with the rest of the regular crew. It's been a while since we've done this. Not since the weekend at the cottage before preseason training started. I'm positive this is everyone's way of keeping me busy, which is smart because I'm definitely not handling this no contact shit well.

I've been stalking Poppy's social media profiles—she hasn't updated even once in the past four days. She doesn't even have a relationship status posted or anything, and I can't remember if there was ever something posted in the first goddamn place.

I've also driven by her work a few times, and by her house once. Mr. Goldberg, her ancient neighbor, was all nice-nice still, loving on me for bringing him oat biscuits. He didn't seem to know anything about what happened with Poppy, just said she'd been out a lot the last few days.

I wonder a bit if the way I am over Poppy is anything like the way Tash is with me. But that can't be possible, because Tash doesn't actually give a shit about me—she just likes to mess with me. I'm in love with Poppy. I know that. I get it now. I just hope it isn't too late, or I think I'm going to be fucked for life.

Alex and Westinghouse have gone to pick up Charlene and the food. Sunny's off feeding the baby somewhere. Or napping. Or maybe both. Randy and Miller are having Xbox wars. Normally, I'd join in, but I'm thinking now is a good time to get some girl advice on how the fuck to proceed. Waiting things out is not my forte.

I've been on the verge of throwing a party the past couple of days, which is a colossally bad idea. Parties equal bunnies and bunnies equal never getting to talk to Poppy again, which is the last thing I want.

I spin my phone on the counter, wishing it would light up with a message. Anything really.

"Why don't you just call her?" Violet asks, popping a cherry tomato into her mouth.

Violet isn't cooking, thank fuck. She really sucks at anything that requires an oven, although I'd never say that to her.

One would think with her math background, measuring ingredients would be easy, but that doesn't seem to be the case. She's too distractible. We're ordering in from a great little Italian place instead. She's making a salad, because that can't be burned.

"She said she needed time."

"Girls always say that. What we really mean is send me all sorts of apology gifts and make the damn problem better."

"Really?" I look to Lily for confirmation. Sometimes Violet's advice is questionable.

Lily shrugs. "It doesn't hurt to send her nice things so she knows you're thinking about her."

"Like flowers?"

"Flowers are always good." Lily nods her approval.

"And chocolate," Violet says.

"I'm allergic to chocolate."

"Really? That's horrible. What about candy? Oh! Alex got my boobs a gift certificate to Victoria's Secret."

"I don't know that I want details about that."

"It's something to consider if she likes lingerie," Violet says.

"Yeah. I don't know if that's really the best idea right now. Flowers seem like they're a safe option. And maybe some candies or something. What else did Waters do when he screwed up?"

"He publicly declared his love for me on a nationally televised interview, and then he stole his own thunder when Chicago won The Cup by asking me to be his girlfriend."

"Uh . . . that's, uh . . . I'm not gonna do that."

"Alex is pretty good at the grand gesture thing."

"What about Ballistic? How'd he fix things?"

"He drove to my house and apologized for being an idiot," Lily says.

"I've already apologized. Now I'm waiting for her to want to talk to me."

"I have an idea!" Violet smacks the counter.

Violet's ideas are sometimes out there, but at this point I'm willing to hear what she has to say.

"You want her to be your girlfriend, right?"

"Aye."

"Do you have any idea how cute you are when you get all leprechaun-y?"

"Leprechauns are Irish. I'm Scottish."

She waves her hand around. "Same thing."

"Not even close," I argue.

"It was supposed to be a compliment. Anyway, back to Poppy and this situation, what do you think the hardest part of dating a hockey player is?"

"Uhhh . . ." I have no idea where she's going with this.

"Going long stretches without sex," Lily says.

Violet gives her a look. "Right. I'm sure you come seven hundred times when you have phone conversations with Balls. Your life is so hard."

"Randy can't make me come on the phone."

"Can we stay on track here?" I ask. Also, I'm not having sex right now, and I don't want to know about the sex my teammates are having.

"I was going to say dealing with rumors and bunnies," Violet says.

"Oh. Yeah. Totally." Lily nods her agreement. "When I moved in with Randy, the bunnies went crazy. For a while there I had daily messages from girls who didn't like that I was with him. They were pretty nasty."

Violet props her chin on her fist. "And how did you deal with that?"

"I talked to Sunny, and you and Charlene, and Randy, of course."

Violet swings her gaze to me, like she expects me to get what the hell the point is, other than if Poppy decides I'm worth dating, she's going to have to deal with bitchy bunnies.

"Poppy needs to meet us."

I frown.

Violet motions to our little group around the island, and then to Randy and Miller in the living room. "We're a family. If you want to get serious with her, you need to bring her into the fold. She needs people to talk to when it gets hard, because it does. I wouldn't have made it through last spring when Alex had his accident without all of you. Alex and I wouldn't even be married. I'd probably still be planning a wedding for eleven million people. If you want Poppy to know you're serious about getting serious, you can't just keep her to yourself. And based on how mopey you are right now, I'm guessing you do want to get serious."

My entire plan has always been to keep her safe from the media crap, but I get what Violet's saying. If this is going to be a real thing, then I can't hide her away.

Lily nods. "Violet's right. Invite her to a game and have her bring a friend. She needs to know that you're invested in something other than her vagina."

THE BIRTHDAY OUTTAKE

WHY DID I WRITE THIS? I wrote this back in 2017 for KU Korner. I loved writing Lance and Poppy's story, and revisiting them in the future, while they're in love and happy and just the sweetest couple ever, made me so happy

BIRTHDAY BASH
GUMMY BEAR STYLE

"Lance is going to jizz a bucketload."

"You should write Hallmark cards," Charlene deadpans while looking at her phone.

Violet makes a face at Charlene. "Eat Darren's dick."

Charlene gives her a saucy grin. "With pleasure."

I cringe at their completely unfiltered banter, thankful we're in my bedroom—the one I share with Lance—and not a public place. I smooth my hands over the soft fabric and check out my reflection in the full-length mirror. "You don't think it's too juvenile?"

"No way. It's freaking adorable," Violet replies.

"I don't want to look adorable. I want to look sexy. Maybe I should change into something else." When I first stumbled on the pinup style, form-fitting dress covered in a gummy bear print pattern, I thought it was hilarious. The mint green fabric is covered in tiny, three-dimensional gummy bears, the sweetheart neckline embellished with forest green lace accents, which also line the hem, and deep green satin ribbon cinches at the waist.

Charlene slips her phone into her purse and crosses her arms over her chest. "You look adorably sexy. You're not changing."

"I think the bra and panties might be overkill." They match the dress. I wish Lily was here, but she's at work and won't arrive until later, and Sunny can't come over until Logan is up from his afternoon nap.

It's not that I don't trust Violet and Charlene's advice. It's just that they're a little forceful about things, especially when they're together. I have a lot of new lingerie and bathing suits thanks to lunch/shopping expeditions with them. I try to say no, but then Violet messages Lance and then he messages me and tells me to put in the credit card he gave me when I moved into his house last year. It's all very kept woman-ish. Except I work full-time as a massage therapist, so I'm not kept at all.

"The bra and panties aren't overkill. Look, you've got this sweet-sexy thing going on." Charlene waves her hand around my face and then gestures to the rest of me. "This dress shows off your curves and it's covered in Lance's favorite gelatin-inspired sugary treat. It's not juvenile and he's going to love it."

"So much that he might jizz in his pants."

"Stop saying *jizz*, Violet. We're not making it the word of the day." Charlene rolls her eyes.

"It's a good word." Violet turns her attention back to me. "All you need is jewelry, something understated and simple, I think."

"What about pearls?" Charlene fingers hers. It's the only necklace I ever see her wear.

Violet and I share a look. "Yeah, pretty sure Poppy here

isn't about to let Lance collar her as a birthday present."

I choke back a laugh. I have no idea what the significance of the pearls are, or what the dynamics of Charlene and Darren's relationship is, but I suspect it's a little unconventional and not in a gummy bear print lingerie/dress kind of way. Apparently, butt plugs were Violet's bachelorette party favor, courtesy of Charlene, which says something.

Charlene throws her hands in the air. "Would you stop?"

"I'm on a wicked roll today, eh?" Violet directs the comment at me.

"You sure are."

Charlene claps her hands together. "Oh! I have a great idea! What about a gummy bear necklace!"

"As cute as that would be, people are going to start arriving in less than an hour. Whatever jewelry I'm wearing needs to come from that box over there." I point to my dresser. I'm throwing Lance a birthday party. A surprise birthday party.

"I mean a real gummy bear necklace," Charlene replies.

"We don't have time for one of your art projects, Char," Violet says.

"Everything we need is right here. It'll only take a few minutes and then you'll be perfect." Charlene gestures to the bed. Instead of rose petals, it's sprinkled with gummy bear confetti, and there are bowls of gummy bears on the nightstand. I make a mental note not to let these two help me plan Lance's next birthday party. But he's turning twenty-five, and I don't think he's ever really celebrated it properly, so here I am, gummy beared out the wazoo.

Charlene roots around in her purse and pulls out a small tube. "What's his favorite flavor?"

"He likes the green ones best. What is this?" I pick up the tube she's tossed on the bed.

"It's an edible adhesive." She starts sifting through the bowl of gummies, piling up all the green ones.

"I'm sorry, it's what?"

"It's like body glue. So you can stick things to your skin. Except it's non-toxic and edible," Charlene explains.

"And you just happen to be carrying that around in your purse?" Violet asks.

"It's handy. It keeps bra straps and other strappy things in place."

Violet grabs the tube from me and inspects it. "It's a little weird that this exists and that it's like, one of your essential items, Char."

"Says the woman who dresses her husband's dick up in costumes."

"That's because Alex's peen is a super hero."

Dear lord, how are these women my friends?

"Okay. Sit here." Charlene pats the comforter.

I sit on the edge of the bed while she and Violet stick gummy bears to my chest in the form of a necklace. I have to admit, when they're done it looks pretty awesome, Also, Charlene has done a good job of drawing attention to my ample cleavage, thanks to the bust line of this dress.

Guests begin to arrive and text messages from Randy inform me of Lance's impending arrival. The boys took him out golfing this afternoon. I've been warned they've already consumed a few beers, so they're all feeling pretty good.

Lance believes we're having a barbeque with a few close friends. He doesn't realize I've invited his entire team to celebrate. It's just after seven when they come rolling in. The house quiets as deep raucous voices fill the foyer.

"Precious! Where ya at?" Lance calls out, his usually light Scottish accent heavier on account of the beers and the sun.

"Just in the kitchen!" I call back, biting my lip as he and the boys round the corner.

The chorus of "surprise" has him stopping in his tracks. His wide-eyed shock turns into a slow grin and he surveys the crowd, scanning until his eyes finally find me. They roam over me in a slow sweep I feel all over my body. He doesn't acknowledge the rest of the room, as if everyone else has ceased to exist.

"I told you he'd ji—" Charlene elbows Violet on the boob before she can finish her sentence.

Lance traces the gummy bear necklace with a fingertip. "These are real, aye." He takes my face in his hands, heedless of the sixty witnesses, and presses his lips to mine. "Ah fuck, ya taste like candy," he mutters, tongue sweeping inside my mouth, tasting the remnants of the gummy bear martini I've been sipping to calm my nerves.

I wrap my hand around his wrists and attempt to disconnect our mouths. I'm sure my face is as red as my name. "We have guests."

He blinks a couple of times, like he doesn't understand, then he looks around, a sheepish grin turning up the corner of his mouth as he raises a hand in greeting. "Everyone make yourselves at home, aye? I just need to speak to my precious Poppy alone for like, twenty minutes, maybe more, depending."

"Lance!" I shriek when he makes like he's going to pick me up and haul me off.

Thankfully, he's just playing. He sets me down and pats my bottom. "This dress is something else," he murmurs in my ear. "I'm going to enjoy taking it off you later."

Later doesn't arrive until two in the morning when the last guest has left. "You threw me a birthday party," Lance says after he closes the door for the final time and sets the security alarm. His accent is still more prominent than usual, although there were an unprecedented number of shots. "No one's ever done anything like that for me."

"I wanted it to be special. Did you have fun?"

"Aye." He cups my face in his hands, dipping down to press a soft kiss to my lips. "But it's been right painful looking at ya all night in this dress and not being able to get you outta it. I'd like to do that now, if that's all right with you."

I smile against his lips. "Aye, that's more than all right."

"Come on then. Let me take ya to bed and show you how grateful I am." He links our pinkies and leads me upstairs.

Lance moves my hair out of the way and kisses my shoulder as he unzips the dress. Coming to stand in front of me, he hooks his fingers in the straps and drags them down my arms, releasing a heavy breath as he takes in the lace-edged bra and panties that match the dress now pooled at my feet.

"Bloody hell, precious. Where the fuck did you find this?" He bites the end of his thumb and shakes his head. "You're a vision." Stepping in close, he runs his fingertips along the edge of the bra, causing a hot shiver to run down my spine. The gummy bear necklace disappeared over the course of the evening, Lance swooping in every once in a while to suck another candy off my chest before whispering into my ear about other things he'd rather be eating.

"I want to worship you for a while." Picking me up, he carries me over to the bed, stripping out of his shirt and pants as he climbs up after me.

His touch is slow and reverent. His kisses are soft and lingering. My bra stays on at first, the cups pulled down, my nipples traced first with light fingertips and then followed by the warmth of his tongue. Lance moves down my body, unhurried, despite the hours spent whispering about how much he couldn't wait to get me up here and naked.

When he reaches my navel, he sits back on his knees, hooks his thumbs into my panties, and drags them down my thighs. "Does this come as a bikini?" he asks, dropping them on the comforter.

"I don't know. I can check."

"Please do." He smooths his hand along the inside of my thighs before shouldering his way between my legs, and then his mouth is on me, laving, slow strokes that push me higher and higher until I unravel.

He prowls back up my body, hips settling between mine, thick erection pressing against me, and then he's easing in, filling me.

His eyes drift shut, and when they open again, his expression is undiluted rapture. He pushes up on one arm, his other palm coming to rest over my heart. "This. You. What you give me. You're the best gift, precious Poppy."

DARREN & CHARLENE

WHY DID I WRITE/INCLUDE THIS? This was meant to be the prologue for Pucked Love. However, it would've revealed very early on Charlene's messed up personal history, which was something I wanted to keep under wraps until later in the story. Writing this helped me frame Charlene's personality and her choices, particularly when it came to her mother and her relationship with Darren. It also would have shifted the storyline quite a bit if she'd fallen in love with the idea of him at fourteen, which isn't quite how things roll out in the actual story.

LOVE AT FIRST SIGHT
Charlene

AN RV IS EQUIVALENT to an unmarked grave. At least in my worst nightmares it is.

Let me explain what that means.

I spent my childhood living in a trailer park. Not the kind where your neighbor is some guy named Billy Bob who wears filthy tanks with horrible huge armholes. The same kind of man who always has a cigarette hanging precariously from between his thin pursed lips while he leers at you and makes you hate the dark and being alone. That wasn't my trailer park experience—although that might've been preferable.

I grew up on The Ranch, which really wasn't a ranch at all. It was hidden away on a desolate patch of Utah dirt, set up with several greenhouses and a dozen or more trailers, full of mostly women I thought were my family. I learned later they weren't.

Everything changed the day I got my first "monthly bleed," otherwise known as a period, Shark Week, or Aunt

Flo's Monthly Visit. But monthly bleed was the phrase of preference at The Ranch. I was fourteen and a half, which is important, that half. I was a late bloomer. Thank heavens for that. I'd been around enough women to know this was part of life, and it signified my transition into womanhood. I still slept with a stuffed animal named Miss Flopsy, so I didn't feel that womanly at the time, but all my sisters made it seem like some kind of rite of passage. I felt gross and ill and my tummy hurt, so I couldn't see what was so awesome about it.

Anyway, the day I went from a fourteen and a half year old to a woman, my entire world changed. In the middle of the night, my mom—who really isn't all there sometimes—stole me away from GHH.

It was all very *Prison Break*. We escaped through a hole in the barb-wire topped fence—I kid you not—and there was even a getaway car, a bag of money, and thank the Lord, an entire backpack of the candies my mom made, day in and day out. They were herbal. Calming. And I pretty much lived on them.

Leaving GHH was both scary and monumental, as it was my first time off The Ranch *ever*. At least that I could remember. And my first time hotwiring a car.

It was traumatic.

It was terrifying.

And an adrenaline rush.

It was also a blessing. But it took me a while to figure that out, too.

I love my mom, but she's a little light on the logic and a few other key elements that make a person rational and capable of good decision-making. Hence the reason we ended up in an unconventional trailer park in the first place.

On our escape trip across central US in an old Volvo that

barely ran and had no heat, I experienced a myriad of firsts. First trip to the grocery store—oh my gosh! So much food in one place and so many things I'd never eaten before. Fruit Loops looked so fun! I was sorely disappointed that they all tasted exactly the same, even though color dictated they should taste different, like Life Savers. First time wearing jeans—so weird to have fabric encasing my legs when I was used to dresses.

But the most memorable of my firsts was two-fold. My first time inside a restaurant and my first exposure to the wonders of television happened in a dingy diner in Omaha, Nebraska on day two of our escape. It was called The Fifth Wheel.

I'll never forget the experience. My mom ordered me chicken fingers, French fries, and chocolate milk from the kid's menu—I was small enough that I looked like a child, even though I wasn't one. I'd never had real chocolate milk, only the kind you make with all the little powder bubble bombs in it, so this was mind-blowing. I was fascinated by the mazes and the word search on the paper menu. And I was allowed to color on it! It held my attention for all of thirty seconds, until I noticed the TV hanging from above the bar.

We'd never had a TV.

Sure I'd seen pictures of the devil's box, but I'd never seen one up close. It didn't look like it held demons inside it, just a moving picture. Kinda neat, really.

On the screen were boys, or men maybe. It was hard to tell since they were so much smaller than in real life and they wore helmets that covered a lot of their faces. They were dressed in bright clothes wearing knife shoes—so crazy!—on their feet and holding sticks.

I recognized the game, sort of. We played a version of

this on The Ranch called ball hockey. But there was no ice and we played in regular shoes. I was pretty good at it. But this was different. These men were fast. They glided down the ice like they had rockets attached to their feet. They were magical.

I read the names on the back of their shirts, curious as to what the numbers below represented. Was it their favorite? Is that how they got it? I was instantly stuck on number twenty-six since that's my birthday. My paper place mat of games was long-forgotten. I dipped fry after fry into the puddle of ketchup on my plate, shoving them into my mouth and chewing as fast as I could so I could stuff another one in. They were so good. And I was hypnotized.

Now I understood why there had been no TVs on The Ranch. I never wanted to stop watching. Maybe that's why it's called the devil's box. It stole away your ability to be productive.

The focus shifted from the ice to the bench where many of the players sat. They weren't always on the ice. They took turns.

In my fourteen and a half years on this planet, I'd had limited exposure to the opposite sex. When number twenty-six came on the screen, I sat forward in my chair. The name Westinghouse spanned his shoulders. It's a long name. He had broad shoulders.

He took a seat on the bench and pulled off his helmet. He shook his head, dark hair dripping wet as he tipped his head back and squirted his water bottle into his open mouth. He used the hem of his shirt to wipe away the beads of sweat trickling down his temples. It was mesmerizing. He was mesmerizing.

Everything about him was fierce. His eyes shifted from

the ice and he looked directly at the screen. The world tilted and spun away. He possessed that kind of severe beauty that stole your breath away. The kind you read about in fairy tales. I couldn't decide if he was the hero or the villain, though.

His eyes were hard like diamonds but the color of pale honey. Like all broken souls, his face was all angles and darkness, encased in sadness.

The darkness and the sadness drew me in. I knew those emotions well. I lived them every day.

When the buzzer went off, he shook his head, like he was erasing whatever was in his head. He shoved his helmet on and surged onto the ice again.

I was fourteen and a half years old when I fell in love with a sport.

I was twenty-two when I met the man who inspired that love, and then I accidentally fell in love with him, too.

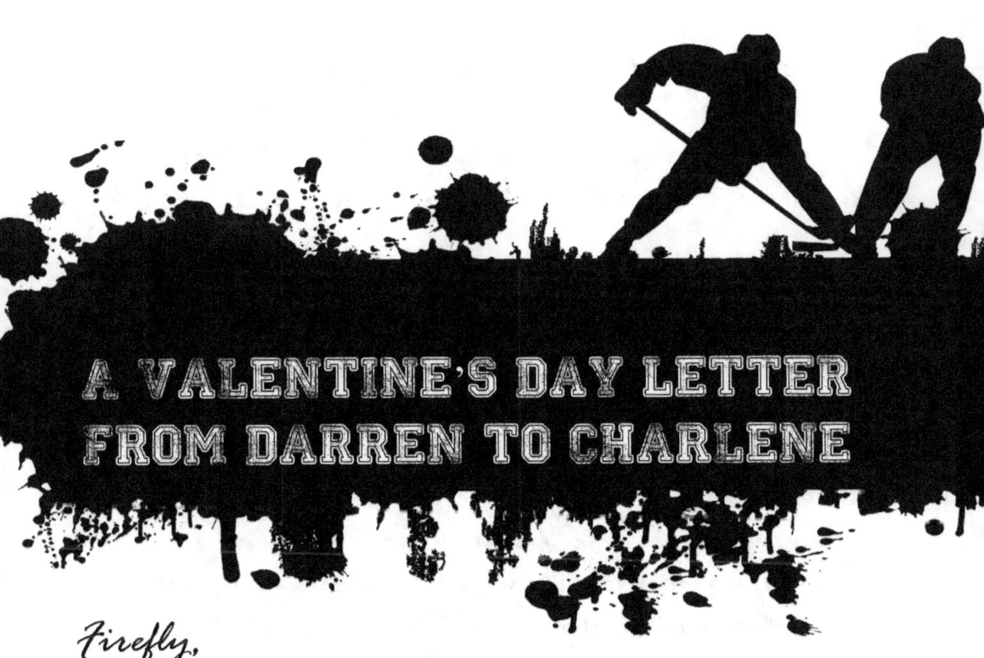

Firefly,

As you know, I'm a highly competitive person. I don't like to lose, especially when it comes to your orgasm challenge nights, which just happens to be one of my favorite games to play with you. I also love Let's See How Long I Can Keep You on the Edge with my Tongue Before You Try to Rip My Hair Out at the Roots.

There is one game I'm terrible at, though, and I've never been happier to suck at something in my life. You wouldn't know this because we've never played, but my inability to play Scrabble is essentially the reason I have you in my life.

If I hadn't lost that game of Scrabble to

Alex, I wouldn't have had to put him up in a suite, they never would have had their one-night stand that lasted forever, and Violet wouldn't have brought you to a game.

Another thing you might not know is that usually my "Resting Asshole Face" is enough to put off most women. For whatever reason, it seemed to have the opposite effect on you. I need to be completely honest with you about that night. I don't remember much of our conversation. All I could focus on was how beautiful you were, and how much I loved the sound of your voice and that I wanted to keep hearing it every day for the rest of my life.

You're the best thing that's ever happened to me, Charlene. Loving you is an honor and I plan to revere you for hours tonight, so don't expect to get much sleep. ;) Happy Valentine's Day, firefly.
My heart is yours,
Darren

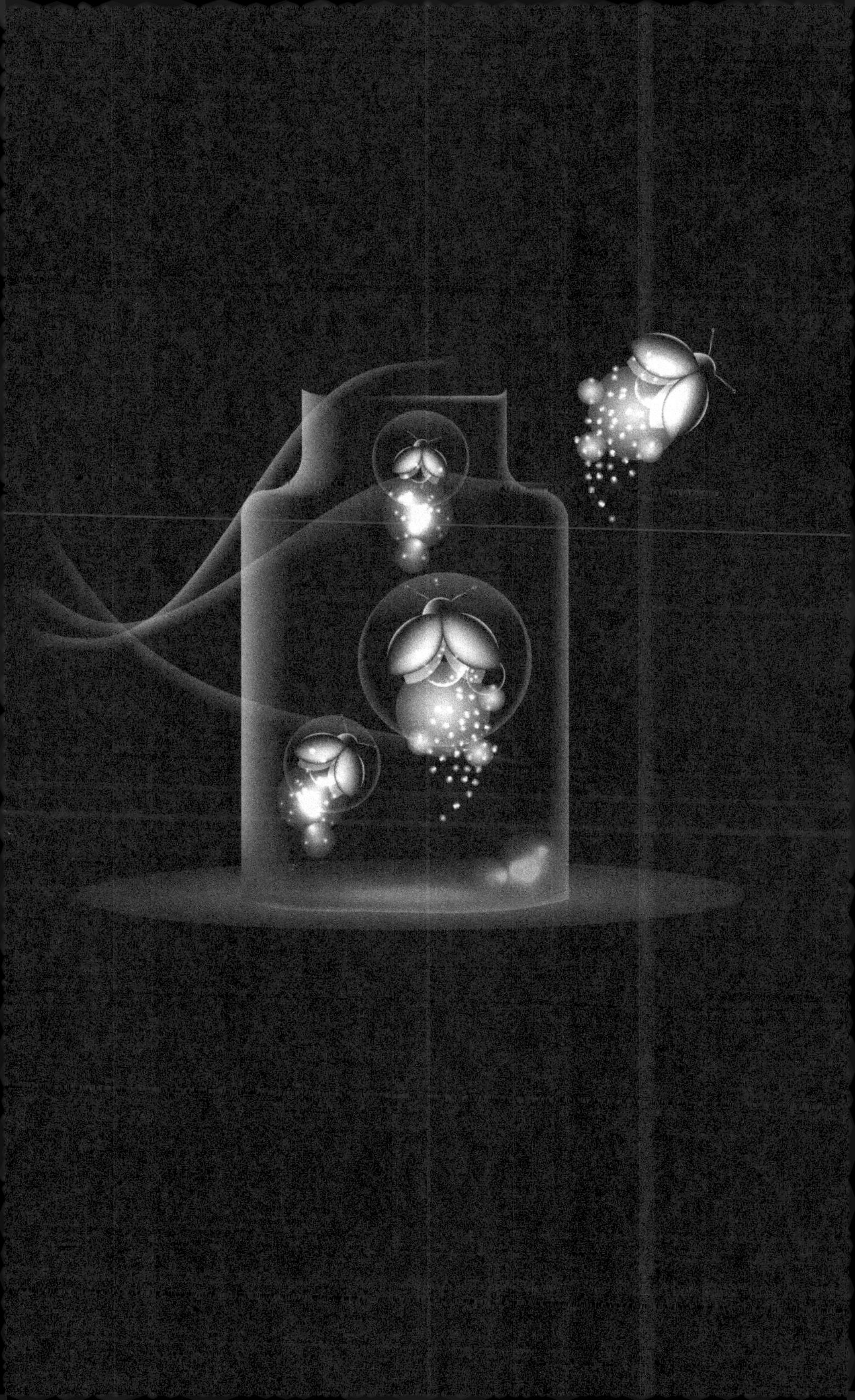